changing tides

AMBER KELLY

ISBN: 979-8-9903206-0-4

Cover Design: Sommer Stein, Perfect Pear Creative Covers
Cover Image: Regina Wamba
Editor: Jovana Shirley, Unforeseen Editing, www.unforeseenediting.com
Proofreader: Judy Zweifel, Judy's Proofreading
Formatter: Champagne Book Design

To Mindi, the best friend a girl could ask for. Loyal, encouraging, and a complete badass. Hurry up and retire already.

changing tides

Enjoy the North Carolina coast!
xoxo,
Amber Kelly

chapter one

WHY THE HELL NOT?

That's the question I ask myself as I open the Tiffany-blue suitcase on my bed and begin to cut the tags off of the pile of new vacation clothes I purchased last week.

I toss them inside, along with my favorite white bikini and pineapple-print cover-up.

Conrad and I planned this vacation for over a year. Painstakingly searching websites for the best accommodations, food, and excursions. I saved every penny earned from my part-time job of waiting tables so we could afford to splurge on anything we wanted to do or buy while in Honolulu on the island of Oahu.

Looking forward to a week of baking in the Hawaiian sun and drinking all the tropical cocktails with my favorite guy was the only thing that kept me going through finals and months of long seven-day workweeks.

Once everything is packed, I snatch the pair of airline tickets from the nightstand and sit on the end of the bed.

Two first-class round-trip tickets for Avie Carrigan and Conrad Sullivan.

Nonrefundable.

I swipe at the warm tear trickling down my cheek.

Pull it together, Avie.

I tuck the ticket with my name on it inside of my purse and tear the one with his name into tiny pieces.

Asshole.

Conrad and I had been dating for almost three years, and stupid me thought maybe he was planning to hide a ring away in his luggage to surprise me on this trip.

It was always the plan. Once I finished school, we would move to the city and begin our life together.

Instead, he took me to dinner last night and professed how much he loved me at the same time he was breaking up with me.

Dumped. The night before the trip of a lifetime.

He said we needed a breather.

I asked, "What the hell does that even mean?"

He explained that his dad's best friend had offered him a job at his architectural firm in New York.

A job that starts next week.

He accepted the position, and he is moving this weekend.

When I asked why the news meant that we needed a breather, he said he wanted to concentrate on work and that a long-distance relationship would be too much of an emotional drain.

"Look, the job is a summer internship. I need to be focused in order to prove myself. After that, I'll know if it's what I want to do and where I want to be. Then, we can revisit our situation and see if we want you to move to New York or if I should move back here to Atlanta."

What he wants to do and where he wants to be?

I stood up as calmly as I could muster, told him he could go fuck himself, picked up the glass of red wine I had been drinking, and dumped it in his lap before I made my way out of the restaurant.

When I made it home, all of his things were gone from the apartment we shared. His clothing, toiletries, laptop, and even the expensive gaming system I'd bought him for his birthday last month.

The jerk had packed up his things while I was on campus. Before bothering to tell me he was moving out.

I will not cry again.

My phone chimes from the dresser, and I stand to see the message that my Uber driver has arrived.

I sling my purse over my shoulder and grab my suitcase.

As I pass the pedestal mirror in the corner of the room, I admire my tanned shoulders peeking out of the top of the gorgeous palm-print maxi dress. I place a large-brimmed straw hat on my head and pull on my new aviator sunglasses before slipping into the white sandals by the door.

Glancing back at the apartment one more time before shutting and locking the door, I head to the elevator.

The driver takes my suitcase and loads it into the back of the car, and I open the door to the back seat, where I find my best friend, Amiya, waiting.

"Hey, chica. I'm ready to get this tropical party started," she squeals as she scoots to the left to make room for me.

Thank God she was able to get off work at the last minute to join me. The romantic getaway I planned will now be the girls' trip of a lifetime. And the best part is that it's being partially funded by the douche formerly known as the love of my life.

"I've been reading the online brochure for the resort." She taps her phone screen and begins to read, "*Welcome to your own private paradise. Our property prides itself on being an exclusive getaway experience, curated just for you. Where you can disconnect from the stress and worries of life, connect to a dream landscape, and enjoy exceptional service with your own personal butler. At The Stanhope Grand Resort, we are all* ohana." She looks up from the device and at me. "That means family."

"I know."

"The pictures are insane. I can't believe we get to stay there," she squeals.

Her enthusiasm is infectious, and I find myself getting excited about the trip.

The driver drops us off, and we make our way to the Delta counter to see if I can get the ticket Amiya purchased upgraded.

"I'm totally okay in coach. Just send me back a free cocktail or two," she says.

"It can't hurt to ask if they can move you beside me. It's not like anyone else will be sitting there."

"But I checked last night, and the cost difference is astronomical," she informs.

I reach into my bag and pull out the American Express card that has my name on it.

"I don't want you to pay for it either."

I grin. "I'm not. This is Conrad's account. He had a card sent in my name a while ago so I could pick up his dry cleaning, grab take-out, and fill his car up with gas on the occasions he was working late. I think the least he can do since he left me with an apartment that still has five months left on the lease is pay for your upgrade."

"Oh, it absolutely is the least he can do," she agrees.

After I explain the situation to the lady at the help desk, she changes Amiya's seat, and we quickly make our way through security.

We grab a bite to eat and a couple of beers at Phillips Seafood while we wait for boarding.

Amiya flirts shamelessly with our barely legal server as I incessantly check my phone.

Once our glasses hit the table, Amiya reaches across the table and snatches my phone from my fingertips.

"Hey!" I quip.

"Hey nothing. You're not going to keep staring at this thing, looking for a text from him or cyberstalking his social media accounts while we're in Hawaii. In less than twelve hours, we're going to be draped in leis and frolicking in paradise. Conrad fucking Sullivan is not going to ruin this trip any further. Got it?"

I nod.

"Let me hear you say it," she insists.

"Conrad fucking Sullivan is not going to ruin this trip," I affirm.

She opens the top of her bag and drops my phone inside.

"You'll get that back when we return home."

"Fine," I huff.

She smiles, picks up her glass, and leans in. "There will be an incredible amount of beautiful men there, and we're going to find one to occupy your time. You'll forget all about what's his name before we return. Here's to a wicked holiday affair."

I raise my glass and clink it against hers. "Cheers."

chapter two

We land at Daniel K. Inouye International Airport and disembark. After claiming our baggage, we are greeted by a couple from the car service Conrad hired, receiving one of the warmest welcomes I've ever encountered. The two are waiting with a sign that reads *Mr. Sullivan and Miss Carrigan.*

I inform them that Conrad was unable to make the trip and introduce them to Amiya.

"Aloha! I am Kiana, and this is my husband, Makoa. We are happy to welcome you to our island," Kiana says as she presents us with colorful necklaces full of blooms, which she places around each of our necks. "This is a fresh flower lei, which is a Hawaiian symbol of aloha, welcome, and love," she explains.

I inhale the fragrance of the beautiful flowers and smile. "Thank you."

Makoa takes our bags and loads them into the back of the car, and then they whisk us away to the private luxury resort.

When we walk through the sliding glass doors, a hotel employee presents us with a tray filled with pink cocktails in fancy glass flutes.

"Aloha," she says as she smiles brightly.

"Aloha to you too," Amiya says as she takes two of the offered glasses.

She follows me as I make my way to the reception desk to check us in.

"Aloha, Miss Carrigan, and welcome to The Stanhope Grand Resort. We have you booked in one of our seaside bungalows for seven nights," the front-desk attendant states.

"That's correct."

"Excellent. I have a key card for you in addition to your mobile access. Please allow Nalani to guide you to your home away from home. A member of our staff will deliver your luggage to you shortly."

She hands me the card, and Amiya and I accompany the young lady who explains the layout of the resort as she walks us down a lit path to the breathtaking bungalow. It has a wall that opens to the beach, allowing us to sleep while exposed to the Pacific breeze and the sound of the crashing waves.

"Wow," Amiya says as we make our way onto the teak deck that leads to the large king-size bed with rose petals sprinkled on top.

A bottle of champagne is chilling in a silver bucket on a tray by the pillows.

She turns to me and raises an eyebrow. "So romantic."

I laugh. "Right?"

Nalani gives us a brief tour of the bungalow and explains how all the gadgets work. There is a remote that lowers the wall and draws the shades and a telephone that can reach our butler directly.

There is an outdoor shower on the deck and a small sauna room off the bath.

"This place is amazing. I might never want to leave," Amiya declares as she plops onto the bed and lies back.

"If only we were independently wealthy," I quip.

Before excusing herself, Nalani informs us that Wednesday's luau begins at six and we can follow the signage on the footpath to the left of our deck to find it.

"What is a luau exactly?" Amiya asks.

"It's a celebration where we feast and drink on the bountiful offerings of the unique crops from this tropical paradise. It is a cuisine you won't find anywhere else in the world. There will be music and dancing, joy and laughter in abundance," she tells us.

"We look forward to it," I declare.

A young boy arrives with our bags ten minutes later. Amiya tips him generously, and he beams as he runs off back to the resort.

We quickly unpack and change into our bikinis before calling the butler, Pika, to arrange our afternoon of sunbathing on the pristine Waikiki Beach, which is steps from our terrace.

When we arrive, our umbrella-covered loungers are prepared just out of reach of the flowing shoreline. Two luxurious, large towels are folded on each one, and sitting atop a table between the two is a plate of fruits and cheeses, along with two cocktails served in coconut shells, adorned with small paper umbrellas.

Pika greets us and asks if there is anything else we need.

"If you keep these yummy coconut concoctions coming, you won't hear another peep from us today," I assure him.

"Yes, ma'am," he promises with a smile before excusing himself.

I lather my body with sunscreen before parking it in the lounger and grabbing my drink.

"So, other than the luau, what's on the agenda for the week?" Amiya asks.

"Tomorrow is the Pearl Harbor tour," I begin.

"Pass," she interrupts.

"What? Why?"

She rolls her eyes. "I know Conrad liked all that history stuff, but I'm on vacation. In Hawaii. I can learn about World War II from a book."

I sigh. "Fine. Tuesday, we're taking the Dole Plantation Tour, and don't you dare say pass," I say as I point at her.

She shrugs. "I'm down with the pineapples."

"Wednesday, we are going snorkeling before the luau. Thursday, we have the island circle bus tour that takes us out to Waimea Valley to see the waterfall, and Friday is the glass-bottom-boat dinner cruise," I continue.

"That's cool," she replies.

"So, we're good for everything, except Pearl Harbor?"

"I'd prefer to lie on the beach all day, every day, working on my tan, and enjoy doing nothing at all but napping, eating, and drinking, but I am here for you, so we'll do all the nerdy, touristy shit that you're excited about too."

I shake my head. "Thanks."

She slides her sunglasses from the top of her head onto her nose. "You're welcome. I'm such an awesome friend."

I laugh. "Yes, you are," I agree.

We both fall silent for about an hour while we soak up the sunshine.

Pika checks in with fresh cocktails in hand.

I take the shells and thank him.

"I could get used to this," I murmur as I pass one of the drinks to Amiya.

"Girl, I could get used to *that* view," she utters, tilting her head toward the water.

My gaze follows hers to the sight where three men with washboard abs, sun-kissed skin, and long, dark hair are sitting astride colorful surfboards.

Oh my.

"You and me both," I mumble.

"Perhaps the best way to get over Conrad is to get under one of them," she suggests.

"Amiya!" I gasp.

"What?" she says with a shrug. "You're young, beautiful, and single. I think a hot Hawaiian fling is exactly what you need."

"They're strangers."

"Precisely. We don't know them; they don't know us. We're like ships passing in the night. No commitment. No expectations." She cuts her eyes to me. "No shared apartment leases. Just temporary adult fun."

That does sound tempting.

"For all we know, they could be here with their wives or girlfriends or boyfriends," I say.

She sets her cocktail aside and stands.

"Where are you going?" I ask.

"We'll never know if we don't ask."

"You're going to ask them if they're single?"

She nods.

"Don't do that. Please," I say as I reach up and grab her wrist, tugging her back to the lounger.

She falls back. "Fine, I won't, but I'm serious. I think a hot and heavy summer fling is just what the doctor ordered," she insists.

"I've never had casual sex before," I confess.

"Never? No one-night stand or quickie in the bathroom at a college frat party?"

"No," I say, feeling the blush hit my cheeks.

"Maybe it's time you did."

"Maybe," I whisper.

She grins, and we bring our straws to our lips as we watch the beautiful boys ride the large waves to the shore.

chapter three

MONDAY AND TUESDAY ARE A BLUR.

I canceled the Pearl Harbor tour, as Amiya had requested, and the two of us spent a blissfully lazy day at a quiet spot on the beach, where we played in the warm water and bathed ourselves in the sunshine. On Tuesday, we spent most of the morning and afternoon on the Dole Plantation Tour, which included a bonus stop at an amazing Arabica coffee tree farm, where I had the best cup of coffee I'd ever tasted, and then we spent the evening on the beach with a bottle of wine as we watched the sun set over the ocean.

Today, we are on a boat, heading out to snorkel and take in all the amazing sea life and coral off the coast of Honolulu.

"Is this okay?" Amiya asks.

I turn to see her standing in the hallway in a teeny-tiny purple bikini. She's wearing gold hoop earrings with a thin gold necklace, two chunky bangle bracelets, and a pair of gold stiletto sandals. A sheer lavender wrap is tied around her waist.

"We're going snorkeling, not yachting with the Kardashians," I quip.

She takes in my outfit—a pair of frayed blue jean shorts, a white bikini, and dark leather flip-flops—and frowns.

"It wouldn't hurt you to add a little pizzazz to your ensemble. Besides, you said we would get back in just enough time to make it to the luau."

We are, but we don't have to get dressed up for that either.

"Haven't you ever watched a movie set in Hawaii? We could run into a handsome singer with soulful eyes at this luau. We have to look our best."

"A handsome singer with soulful eyes?"

She shrugs. "I might have watched *Blue Hawaii* during our flight."

"Trust me, Elvis isn't going to be at our table," I state.

"Maybe not, but that doesn't mean other handsome Hawaiian natives won't be. Jason Momoa lives here."

I roll my eyes. "Jason Momoa is probably on some set in Hollywood."

"Will you just change?" she huffs.

"Relax. I brought a couple of gorgeous tropical maxi dresses. I plan to slip one on before dinner, but seriously, you can't wear those shoes on the boat."

She goes to the bedroom and returns, sans jewelry and wearing a pair of flat pearl-white sandals.

"Better?"

"Much," I reply.

When we arrive, the boat *Coral King* is waiting in slip B-3 at Huaka'i Basin Boat Harbor on Waikiki.

After a short safety presentation, we are all fitted with life jackets and equipment before boarding the craft. We set sail for a snorkeling site in Turtle Canyons, where Hawaiian green sea turtles congregate above the reef.

"Do you think one of them would give me mouth-to-mouth

if I were to drown?" Amiya asks as her chin lifts to the crew in red swim trunks, seated across from us on the boat.

One is helping a small child strap on the flippers the excursion provided.

"I knew I should have worn my sexy shoes," she whispers.

I elbow her side.

"You are," I say as I raise my right leg and wiggle my foot, which is wrapped in orange rubber.

She starts to giggle when her eyes go wide. She does her best ventriloquist impersonation when she speaks without moving her lips. "Oh my God, one's coming over here."

I turn my head to see one of them approaching us, and I start to greet him when my long flaxen hair is caught in the breeze coming off the cerulean water and obstructs my view. By the time I have it contained by a ribbon, he has passed by and taken a seat next to the tour guide, Alex, at the back of the boat. He is staring in our direction, and his lips lift in a sexy half smile.

"I'm so glad you made me do this," Amiya says.

When the engine comes to a stop, Alex stands and instructs us all to create a single-file line.

With my snorkel gear in hand, I feel a tingling mix of excitement and anticipation as we follow the others who drop from the steps of the vessel into the ocean, one by one.

I adjust my mask and fins, and my heart races when it's my turn to leap.

Taking a deep breath, I close my eyes and drop. I keep them closed until I feel the cool embrace of the sea enveloping me and kick my way to the surface just as Amiya takes the handsome crew member's hand and lets him help her down.

Once she is by my side, we swim to the others who are skimming the water.

Alex explains what we will see and the boundaries we are to adhere to as he makes his way into the center of the group. Then, we have forty-five minutes to explore the roped-off area on our own.

Amid the vibrant coral formations and the kaleidoscope of colorful tropical fish, the giant green sea turtles swim so close to us that we can almost reach out and touch them.

I am in complete awe.

My only complaint is that the crowd is so large, and as other boats come close to the reef, their parties join us in the water.

We are literally elbow to elbow by the time the last vessel anchors.

I am skimming the rippling water, watching a spinner dolphin playing just outside the ropes when a figure catches my eye.

A man with a muscular back and a mop of unruly, dark hair is swimming effortlessly through the water. I watch as he gracefully navigates around the other explorers, his movements fluid and mesmerizing. When he surfaces, I recognize the playful blue eyes behind his mask. It's one of the guys who was surfing the day we arrived.

My attention is pulled from him as a flying fish emerges and crashes back down in front of me, and I let out a surprised scream.

"Avie, are you all right?"

I hear Amiya's concerned voice, and I turn to see her wading with Alex and his coworker.

"I'm fine," I shout.

I'm about to swim to them when a voice interrupts my movement.

"Looks like someone wants to be friends," the man says with a chuckle, his eyes crinkling at the corners as he grins.

The little fish flies out of the water again and splashes water in my face as he lands by my chest.

"Well, he's an awfully persistent thing, isn't he?" I reply playfully.

He laughs, and it echoes through the water.

"Absolutely. But I can't say I blame him. Showing off for a pretty girl."

My heart skips.

He paddles toward me and stops once he reaches my side, water droplets glistening on his skin.

"I'm Sebastian, by the way," he says, extending a hand.

"Avie," I reply, shaking his hand with a smile.

"Didn't I see you on the beach the other day?" he asks.

"I'm not sure. Maybe," I lie. "My friend and I arrived on the island on Sunday."

"Where are you staying?" he asks.

"At The Stanhope Grand Resort on Waikiki."

He grins. "Yeah, I'm sure it was you."

"We did notice some guys surfing. Was that you?"

He bites his lip and nods. "Yep, me and my buddies are here to catch some waves for a few days before heading back home."

I open my mouth to ask where home is when a whistle sounds, drawing our attention to Alex standing aboard the *Coral King*.

"I think that means my time is up," I mutter, disappointment in my voice.

I slide my eyes back to his.

The sun has dipped lower, casting a warm amber glow over the water.

"It was a pleasure to meet you, Avie."

"Same," I say.

He kicks his feet and begins to float away on his back.

"I hope we run into each other again," he bellows, and a flutter of excitement dances in my chest at the sound of his deep voice.

"Maybe we will," I call back.

I swim over to the boat and take Alex's hand as he helps me climb aboard. I grab a towel from the basket on the right and wrap it around myself. I pluck the fins from my feet and walk to the bench seat where Amiya is chatting with the hot crew guy.

"Hey, I lost you out there," she says as I take a seat.

"Did you have a good time?" I ask.

She leans in and wraps an arm around my shoulders. "The best," she squeals.

"Me too."

chapter four

WHEN WE STEP ONTO THE SANDY SHORE AND NAVIGATE the footpath, the distant sounds of drums and laughter are carried by the ocean breeze.

I can't help but feel a sense of excitement as Amiya and I make our way toward the sounds.

We showered after the snorkeling excursion and took a long nap in the hammocks on our deck before dressing for tonight.

I skipped makeup, except for swiping on some lip gloss, and spritzed on a moisturizing mist. Then, I pulled my beach-wave hair into a long ponytail and slipped on a strapless, vibrantly colored maxi dress and sandals.

The Hawaiian luau is in full swing when we make it to the venue.

We take a few moments to mingle with the crowd and take in the enchanting music and festive dancers.

The tantalizing aroma of grilled food fills the air as we take a spot at a communal table.

We settle in and watch the fire dancers mesmerize the gathering.

That's when I notice him.

My eyes meet Sebastian's across the crowd, and he and his two friends make their way over to us.

He stops across the table and smiles.

"Hi. Sebastian, isn't it?" I ask.

"Yes. It's nice to see you again, Avie."

We stare at one another for a long moment when a throat clears.

I look over at Amiya's expectant face.

"Oh, this is my friend Amiya. Sebastian and I met while snorkeling this afternoon," I explain.

She raises an eyebrow.

"And this is Parker and Anson," Sebastian introduces.

"Mind if we join you?" Anson asks.

Amiya extends her arm to the empty seat across from us. "Not at all."

The three of them sit down, and with the rhythmic beat of the drums in the background, we strike up a conversation.

"What brings you fellas to Oahu?" Amiya asks.

"Work," Parker says.

"Work? I thought you guys were just catching some waves for a few days," I say to Sebastian.

"That too. We work on a couple's personal yacht in the summers, traveling from California to Hawaii. I am the captain, and these two are part of my crew."

"You sail a yacht from California to Hawaii?" I say.

"Yep, every summer for the past four years. They're originally from the east coast. We grew up with the grandson. Now, they have a home in Los Angeles and one here on the island where they like to bring friends and their kids on vacation."

"How long does it take to sail from California?" Amiya asks.

"It takes two weeks at sea to get here. They usually stay two to three weeks, and then we sail them back," Sebastian explains.

"So, your entire summer is bringing them here and taking them back?" I ask.

"Pretty much, but they pay us very well, and we get to stay on the yacht for free while we're on the island. So, it's a sweet deal," Parker replies.

"Damn, that's a cool gig," Amiya says. She looks at me. "It sure beats waiting tables all summer."

"Where are you ladies from, and what brings you to Oahu?" Anson asks.

"We're from Atlanta, and we both attend the University of Georgia. We'll be graduating next spring," Amiya answers.

Parker leans back in his chair. "I knew it. I knew I heard a sweet Southern accent."

We fall into an easy rapport as we are served a delicious feast of poi, fish, roasted kalua pig, limu, breadfruit, sweet potatoes, lau lau, opihi, and a selection of fresh fruits and haupia.

As the night wears on, we find ourselves on the dance floor.

Our laughter mingles with the music as Amiya and I try our hand at hula dancing, following the instructions of the locals.

The boys join us, and before I know it, Sebastian and I are moving in harmony, our bodies swaying to the melody. In that moment, it feels like the crowd has faded away, leaving only the two of us.

As the luau reaches its end, we steal away to the shoreline with our bellies full of wonderful food and cocktails in our hands.

The moon's soft glow illuminates the waves, casting a magical spell upon the beach.

Sebastian and Anson build a fire, and we sit and enjoy the night breeze and the sound of the waves meeting the sand.

Parker receives a text from a girl he met earlier in the week, and he and Anson talk Amiya into accompanying them to the tiki bar a few miles down the beach.

"You sure you don't want to come? It's still early," Amiya asks.

I shake my head. "Nah. I just want to stay and enjoy the moonlit beach a while longer," I say.

"I'll stay and keep her company."

Her eyes slide to Sebastian, and she smiles.

Then, she turns back to me and leans down to whisper in my ear, "Remember what I said about getting under a hot stranger."

I push her away, and she winks at me.

"All right, you two kids have fun. Don't do anything I wouldn't do," she says as she follows the guys, and I watch them fade out of sight.

"They'll take good care of her. You don't have to worry. Trust me," Sebastian assures.

They should be the ones worried.

I turn back to him and smile. "I do."

And it's true. I just met him, but for some reason, I do trust him.

It's probably the cocktails.

"What do you say to a night swim?" he asks.

"I do have my bathing suit on under my dress," I muse.

He stands and offers me his hand.

I take it, and he helps me to my feet.

He watches intently as I shimmy out of my dress, letting it fall to the sand.

Then, I take off running toward the water, and he gives chase.

I dive into the dark depths of the ocean, and when I surface, Sebastian is at my side.

He wraps an arm around my waist and tugs me close.

Before I have a chance to overthink, I bring my lips to his.

His hands slip down to my ass, and he hoists me up onto his hips. My legs wrap around him as his teeth nip at my bottom lip, and I gasp.

Taking the opportunity, he deepens the kiss, and my fingers slip into the wet hair at his nape, holding on.

When we finally come up for air, I drop my legs and release him. Then, I slip back into the water and take off under the rushing waves.

He catches up to me in minutes, and when he reaches out to clasp my waist again, I twist and kick, splashing water in his face.

Squealing, I attempt to slip past him, but I can't escape his firm grip.

Finally, I give in and slip my arms around his shoulders.

"You're beautiful, Avie," he whispers against my skin.

I rest my forehead against his and let him hold me.

An electric current runs between us, and I can feel his cock twitch as my heat brushes against him.

I gasp, and his eyes widen slightly as his lips part.

I can feel the loud thump of my heart beating in my chest as my breath quickens.

I can hear Amiya's voice in my head.

"A hot and heavy summer fling is just what the doctor ordered."

I go still as the water laps around us.

"Avie?"

I bring my eyes to his, and my legs tighten around him, my core nestling against his erection.

That's all it takes.

He brings his lips to my shoulder and peppers a trail of kisses to my collarbone as he walks us back to the shoreline.

I toss my head back to give him better access, which causes my chest to press into his.

The thin, wet fabric of my bikini leaves nothing to the imagination.

He marches us up the steps to the dock that leads to the yacht as he cups one breast with his hand and gently kneads it.

I close my eyes and moan, and we walk aboard the yacht and down a hallway that leads to a small bedroom.

He kicks the door shut behind us, and we fall onto the small double bed.

He lets go of me long enough to reach around, undoing the straps tied at my neck, and pulls the white fabric down.

Plump pink nipples greet him.

"Fuck," he groans.

He sucks one between his teeth and gives it a rough tug. I buck off the bed, and he releases it, licks it gently, and blows across it. It tightens to a hard peak, and he wraps his lips around it once more.

My hips start to rock into him, and as soon as I find the contact my body is searching for, I hasten my movement.

The friction feels so good as I slide up and down on him.

His mouth moves to the other breast and sucks it as I continue to glide against his eager cock.

When I can take no more, I reach between us and into his trunks.

He bites down on my nipple, and I gasp.

I wrap my fingers around him and pull him free.

"Give me your mouth, Avie," he commands.

I lean in and do just that.

Our tongues wrestle as I continue to caress him.

His hand shimmies down and brushes across my core.

I bite my lip, and my body trembles as he slides a finger inside my bottoms, where he finds my entrance wet and ready, and begins to pump it in and out slowly.

His head falls to my shoulder, and I take all of his weight as I lose myself to the pleasure.

"Oh God," I groan.

I release him, hook my thumbs into the band of his shorts, and tug them down.

He bears up so I can slide them down his legs, and then he kicks them onto the floor. Then, he slides my bottoms down my thighs.

He takes hold of his cock and guides it to my opening, and his eyes come to mine, searching for permission.

I raise my hips to meet him, and he slides inside of me.

It feels so damn good as he thrusts forward, picking up the pace and going deeper and deeper until he fills me completely.

My muscles begin to tighten around him, and I scream his name as he finds my clit and circles it with his thumb, applying just the right amount of pressure I need.

I circle my hips and move more urgently, seeking the release my body wants so badly.

My legs tense around him, and I begin to shudder as I get closer.

"Look at me, Avie," he commands.

My head snaps up, and he watches as I lose the battle and shatter around him.

My cries fill the cabin and echo against the walls.

Then, he stiffens atop me, and his cry mingles with mine as I milk his orgasm from him.

It's the guttural sound.

His head stays buried in my neck as our breathing calms.

When he finally looks up, he asks, "Are you okay?"

I nod.

He brings his hand to the side of my face and cups my cheek.

Then, he leans down and kisses me gently.

"That was incredible," he whispers against my lips.

Then, he falls to the side, tugs me into his chest, and pulls the covers over us.

Before I can even wrap my head around what just happened, I hear the rhythmic panting of his breath in my ear, and I know he has fallen asleep.

Carefully, I untangle myself from his arms and climb quietly from the bed.

I gather my suit and tiptoe out into the hallway of the boat and shut the door gently.

Then, I make my way back to the beach to gather my dress and sandals and head back to my bungalow.

chapter five

I AWAKEN TO THE SOUND OF THE COVERS RUSTLING AND THE FEEL of Amiya climbing in bed beside me.

I peek over at her. "What time is it?" I ask.

"Six in the morning," she mumbles.

I blink against the sunlight bathing the deck and sit up.

"Are you just coming in?" I ask.

"Yeah, I ran into the hunky crewman from the *Coral King* at the bar, and the two of us took a bottle of rum and a couple of beach towels to the shore and made good use of it all. I woke up with a pounding head and sand in all the wrong places," she grumbles.

"That's going to cause some uncomfortable chafing," I say as I plop back and pull the duvet up to my chin.

"Worth it," she says.

"We're not going to make it to the waterfall today, are we?" I ask.

She opens an eye and looks at me. "Nope."

I shrug. "I'm good with that."

The truth is, I'm exhausted. Deliciously so.

We snuggle in and drift off to the sound of the light rain that has begun to fall on the deck.

And I dream of sailing the open seas on a yacht with a beautiful stranger.

I awaken to ringing coming from somewhere in the bungalow.

I roll over to see Amiya is still dead to the world.

The ringing stops, and I sit up and swing my legs over the edge of the bed.

Standing, I make my way to the bathroom.

The ringing starts again, and I follow the sound to the coat closet in the foyer beside the door.

I open it as the ringing stops and then starts once again.

I find Amiya's bag and fish the phone out just as it stops again.

The screen illuminates, and the wallpaper of me and my parents smiling stares back at me with a notification of six missed calls.

All from Conrad.

What the hell does he want?

I turn off the ringer so it doesn't wake up Amiya and carry the phone into the kitchen with me.

I debate on whether or not I should return the calls.

What if it's an emergency?

The thought crosses my mind just as a text comes through.

I read it and freeze at his words.

Amiya emerges from the bedroom, yawning and rubbing the sleep from her eyes.

"I need some hair of the dog," she mutters, stopping short when she sees my face.

Her eyes fall to the phone in my hand.

"What's wrong?" she asks.

I burst into tears.

She rushes to me and wraps her arms around me.

"I think I made a mistake," I whimper.

The phone slips from my hand, and she reads the message from Conrad.

"Fuck me," she hisses before dropping it onto the counter.

She lets me cry into her chest for a few more minutes, and then she leans back.

"Let's go get some breakfast and talk about it," she suggests.

"Okay."

I sniffle, and she wraps an arm around my shoulders and leads me to the bedroom to get dressed.

I let Amiya talk me into taking the rest of our days in Hawaii to get my head together and decide what I want my future to look like.

Since I was a little girl, it has been my dream to graduate with a degree in marine science and apply for a job as an aquarist at the Georgia Aquarium.

Is that still what I want in life?

She doesn't leave my side as we take the glass-bottom boat tour.

I stare down at the natural beauty at our feet.

This is what I love. The ocean. The sea life.

We spend our last day on the island on the beach with Pika serving our breakfast, lunch, and dinner in our cabana.

I decide to stay at the bungalow and spend time in the sauna as Amiya gets dressed and attends the final party at the resort.

I don't want to risk running into Sebastian. I wouldn't know what to say to him. I snuck out that night without even leaving a note.

It was for the best.

We hadn't exchanged phone numbers, and we don't even know each other's last names. Our night of passion will forever be a beautiful memory of my time here in paradise, but that's where it needs to stay.

In my memory.

When Amiya returns, she informs me that there was no sign of Sebastian or the other guys, so I guess he feels the same way about our brief tryst.

The next morning, we pack and say goodbye to our cozy bungalow as Pika comes to help us with our things and loads us into a car.

"Thank you for everything," I tell him as I wrap him in a tight hug.

"You're very welcome, Miss Carrigan. I hope your life journey leads you back to Oahu one day," Pika says as he returns my embrace.

"Me too."

The driver whisks us away to the airport, and we get checked in for our flight and make our way to the waiting plane.

I take my seat beside the window and stare out at the island as Amiya holds my hand.

Goodbye, palm trees and blue seas.

We were only here for a week, and yet it felt like a lifetime. I'm not the same girl who boarded the plane in Atlanta.

This island changed me.

I fish my phone from my purse as Amiya chats away with the gentleman across the aisle.

Tapping the screen so I can place it into Airplane mode before tucking it in the back of the seat in front of me, I pull up the text from Conrad one more time.

Conrad: I miss you so damn much. I'm sorry. I fucked up. Please come to New York.

New York …

chapter six

Avie

Present Day—Five Years Later

"Here we go. The key sticks a bit, so you just have to wiggle it in the lock."

I follow the elegant older woman with silver hair up the cobblestone path from the street to the covered porch of the weathered coastal cottage. Her brightly colored kaftan gently flows around her on the breeze, carrying the scent of jasmine.

The house sits on a tranquil lot by the water. It's quite the change from the sleek, modern SoHo apartment that we've called home for the past four years, with its dark-pitched roof, robin's-egg-blue clapboard siding, and dormer windows.

As the owner, Sabel Hollister, leads me up the three steps to the front door, I note how the sun-bleached appearance of the fading paint only adds to the house's character.

My attention is drawn to the small garden situated to the left. It's overgrown with beach grass and lavender hydrangeas, weighted with spring blooms that are dancing in the cool afternoon breeze.

"I'll have my husband, Sebby, come by and oil it for you after he gets home from work this evening," she says as she pushes the heavy oak door open and guides me into the foyer, which opens to the intimate and cozy living area with a low ceiling, exposed beams, and hardwood floor.

"Welcome to Sandcastle Cottage. The home comes furnished,

of course. If you have personal items you'd like to use instead, we can have our furniture moved to storage," Sabel explains.

The vintage furnishings are ideal for the space, as is the decor, featuring nautical-themed pieces and maritime artifacts. Together, it all evokes a sense of seaside charm and nostalgia. Just what I was looking for.

I shake my head.

We'll only be here in Sandcastle Cove for six months, the length of my contract with The North Carolina Sea Turtle Project, working in conjunction with the Sandcastle Cove Sea Turtle Rescue and Rehabilitation Center.

"No, it's perfect," I whisper.

Sabel smiles as she looks around the room.

"It is, isn't it? Sebby and I lived here the first few years of our marriage. Oh my, that was fifty years ago now, before our little family outgrew it and he built the one we live in now. A lot of good memories were made within these walls. We didn't have the heart to let it go, so we've been using it as a seasonal rental ever since," she explains.

She guides me around the layout of the two-bedroom, one-bath cottage and to the French doors just beyond the table in the kitchen.

"This is my favorite spot," she says as she opens the doors.

We walk out to the large screened-in porch that overlooks the cove. A lush, thick rug covers the wood-plank decking. An outdoor sectional sofa with a palm-tree print is situated to the left, surrounding a driftwood coffee table. Two large wicker rocking chairs are to the right, facing the water.

"This view is something else," I gasp as I take in the spectacular vista.

"It's the best place to enjoy your morning coffee or afternoon cocktail," she continues.

An old wooden door leads out to a set of stairs that descends to a path of stepping stones, making their way to a pier that juts out into the water with a covered seating area and boat ramp.

"You have use of the pier as well. It's private and quiet most days, though don't be startled if my grandson docks his boat occasionally. He likes to park it over here and walk over to our house from time to time. Let me know if it bothers you."

"I'm sure it will be fine. I don't have a boat."

"Still, the pier is nice for fishing, crabbing, and even sunbathing."

"I'll keep that in mind," I reply.

We walk the property, and she gives me the rundown of the plant varieties in the fenced-in garden with its rows of blooms, a green metal table with two high-back chairs, and wooden A-framed swing.

"My daughter is going to be over the moon. When I showed her the photos online, she was elated at the prospect of having our very own fairy garden," I tell her.

She turns and smiles.

"Really? You know, I've been after Sebby to remove the trunk of that old oak tree that was lost to a tropical storm a few years ago, but I could have him hollow it out and add a door and rooftop," she offers.

"Oh, no, I don't want you to go to all that trouble. Leia will just enjoy having tea parties at the garden table and lying on a blanket among the flowers," I say, but I can see the blueprints taking form behind her eyes as she waves me off.

"No trouble at all. My great-grandchildren would love it. Oh, I can't wait to talk to my daughter, Milly, about it. We love a project. Speaking of, when will your little girl be joining us?"

"Next weekend. She's in Atlanta with my parents, but my friend Amiya is driving her up on Saturday."

"That gives us plenty of time to plot," she squeals.

"Thank you, Sabel. I truly appreciate you accepting the extended lease."

In my research, I found that most of the rentals available on the island during the season are short-term only, and all long-term were already spoken for. When I saw this listing, I fell in love with it. I decided to take a shot and send the owners an email, explaining our circumstances and asking if they'd consider letting us rent it for six months.

She reaches out and takes my hand. "You're more than welcome. Besides, Sebby is thrilled not to have a parade of renters this year. Less work for him."

We head back to the street to where my leased candy-apple-red Corvette convertible is parked.

I know the gas-guzzling, two-seater car is not a practical vehicle for a single mother, but I saw it on the lot and decided I wanted a fun car for the summer at the beach.

Sabel hands me the key chain with the house key and a pink leather flamingo attached.

Another silver-haired lady appears from the house neighboring the cottage and makes her way to the mailbox at the top of her drive.

Sabel raises her hand in greeting. "Good afternoon, Ida Mae," she calls.

"Hi, Sabel," she returns.

"This is Avie. She and her daughter, Leia, will be your neighbors until November," Sabel introduces.

"That's Ida Mae. She makes the best apple pie on the island. I'm sure you'll be finding one on your porch any day now."

I wave to the woman, and she returns the gesture before disappearing back down the driveway.

"Oh, before I forget, there's a white golf cart in the garage. The key is hanging on a hook by the door for our grandson, but you add it to that key chain. The cart is electric and road-certified. You're welcome to use it while you're here. You are allowed to drive it everywhere on the island as long as you wear your seat belt and obey the traffic laws. It has a resident sticker, so you get preferred parking at all beach accesses, The Point, and the local shops. Just charge it at night, and it will run all day long."

"That's amazing. Thank you."

And it will save gas money.

She wraps me in a warm hug.

"We're happy to have you with us, and I can't wait to meet your little one. If you need anything, we are just a phone call or two minutes away."

I watch as she makes her way across the cul-de-sac and toward the stilted houses across the way.

To be honest, I wasn't sure we'd enjoy spending the summer and fall on this tiny island off the southern coast of North Carolina, but I needed the work, and the distance from the city and my ex-husband will be refreshing.

If everyone is as welcoming as our new landlord, Sandcastle Cove might just be the haven we need to figure out what's next for me and my girl.

chapter seven

Avie

"SANDCASTLE COVE HAS EIGHTEEN MILES OF SHORELINE. WE survey every mile each morning from May until November, looking for sea turtle tracks and nests. Once a nest is identified, it is marked and roped off. We rotate weeks, so you'll be on the schedule with the others. It will be emailed to you at the beginning of each month."

I follow Kimball, the program director at the Sandcastle Cove Sea Turtle Rescue and Rehab Center, as she shows me around the facility.

"And nights?" I ask.

"Nights?"

"I assume we have to patrol and protect nests."

She shakes her head. "When a nest is close to boiling, we keep a close watch, but we have a large family of volunteers who help monitor identified nests. They report any unlawful activity, and they call us in the event we are needed. We make the call to authorities if their assistance is required. Your number will be added to the emergency contact list. Other than that, we will keep an observation at night if there is an increase of heavy rainfall or storm surges in the forecast," she explains.

"Got it."

"Don't worry, Avie; the residents here on the island are very conscious and protective of the sea turtles. We rarely have any problems, apart from the occasional uninformed or inebriated tourist. And even they usually leave the marked nest alone. We just have to make sure they fill in any holes they dig in the sand and that they don't use bright flashlights to chase crabs on the beach at night near the nests."

Successfully digging themselves from the nest is only the first obstacle new hatchlings face. They have to safely make the march from the nest to the sea, avoiding birds, crabs, and other animals, holes in the sand, and artificial light from beachcombers and beach houses that can disorient them and cause them to head in the wrong direction instead of following the light from the moon and stars to the ocean.

The stretch of beach the hatchlings have to navigate to the water is a virtual minefield, and once they do make it to the safety of the sea, they have to fight birds, dolphins, sharks, and many species of carnivorous fish to make it to adulthood. A feat that only one in every thousand achieves. Compound that with the threats to adult sea turtles—illegal harvesting, pollution, oil spills, habitat degradation and encroachment, coastal development, climate change, et cetera—and this is why they are on the endangered species list and we must fight so hard to save them with conservation efforts.

"You'll spend most days here at the research center running labs on soil and water samples, helping with our children's education program, and assisting in the hospital, where we accept and rehab three types of turtles—loggerhead, green, and Kemp's ridley—from all over the state. We also take in patients from other states on a case-by-case basis," Kimball continues.

This is my first time working with sea animals. My career in marine science has been limited to research behind a desk at the New York State Department of Environmental Conservation. But I've always wanted to be hands-on with aquatic animals and habitats.

I'm excited for this new adventure even if it's only a seasonal contract.

Kimball finishes the tour and supplies me with my credentials and the standard embroidered polo-shirt-and-white-shorts uniform.

"Thank you, Avie. We look forward to having you on the team."

"Thank you. I'm excited to get started," I reply.

"See you in two weeks. This is going to be a great season," she declares.

I lower the roof on the Corvette and throw a ball cap on my head and sunglasses on my nose as I make my way down Beach Avenue.

The rows of beachfront homes that sit a few feet away from the barrier of the dunes are an array of pastel colors with kitschy names, like Seas the Day and Conched Out. My favorite by far is the gorgeous aqua oasis, aptly named Reel Broke.

Sandcastle Cove has a beautiful coastline, but the island offers amenities far beyond the beach itself, such as boating, kayaking, fishing, golfing, and both casual and fine dining. It has established retail and unique, small, local shopping; the wharf and marina; two fishing piers, one on either side of the island; an active town recreation center, as well as a public library, and several well-maintained family and dog parks … all watched over faithfully by the Sandcastle Cove Lighthouse for the past sixty-six years.

As I make my way toward the far end of the island, I notice there aren't any large resorts or high-rise hotels in sight. Just a couple of boutique hotels and affordable seaside motels sprinkled among the beach houses. None of which are over three stories in height, preserving the view of the homes on the second and even third row from the ocean.

I also have a hard time locating a grocery store. When I spot a tiny market near the bustling marina, I pull into the lot and park.

People are milling about with fishing poles and coolers. Trucks are sitting patiently, awaiting their turn to back their trailers into the allotted public boat access points. Vessels of all shapes and sizes—from small wooden fishing boats to impressive yachts—dot the pier.

I grab my wallet from the console and make my way into the market, where there is a fresh seafood counter, butcher, a small locally sourced produce section, and a limited array of shelf, household, and pharmacy items. In the back of the store, there is a bait-and-tackle shop with a line of boardshorts-clad men juggling cases of beer and bags of ice.

Not exactly what I'm used to, but I embrace the coastal small-town charm as I claim a woven basket from the stand by the door, and I load up on items to stock the kitchen before Amiya and Leia arrive tomorrow morning.

"Hi, looks like someone is planning a feast," the cashier says as she unloads my wares.

"With no McDonald's or Taco Bell within twenty-five miles of the island, it looks like I'm going to be doing my fair share of cooking while I'm here," I explain.

"Yeah, we prefer the local businesses get our money. But trust me, the Barnacle Café and Sandcastle Cove Deli are amazing if a quick, cheap bite is what you're looking for," she says.

"I'll remember that."

"How long are you in town?" she asks.

"About six months. I'll be working with the sea turtles this season."

"Great. Well, welcome to Sandcastle Cove. We love the turtles around here. And there are plenty of food spots, including amazing food trucks down at the wharf," she continues.

"It's on my list to explore when my daughter arrives."

"How old is she?"

"She just turned four," I reply.

"She's gonna love it here. There's so much for kids to do. Veterans Park has a pirate's ship and splash pad."

She finishes totaling my purchases, and I thank her and pay before taking the brown paper bags and carrying them to my car.

I set it in the passenger seat and bring my hand to cover my eyes as I squint at the glistening water.

Wow, this place is breathtaking, and everyone is so friendly.

I can't wait for my girl to arrive. It's going to be a magical summer.

chapter eight

Avie

WHEN I PULL INTO THE DRIVEWAY, I SEE THAT THE GATE to the garden is open.

Sebby and his friend, Donnie Dale, have spent the last three evenings working on the oak tree. Meticulously hollowing the broken trunk and sanding it to smooth perfection so that a precocious four-year-old can hide inside safely and comfortably.

I carry the groceries to the stoop and make my way over to the fence.

"Hi, Sebby," I call.

His balding head pops up from his tools, and he turns a leathery smile to me as he removes the towel hanging from the back pocket of his worn jean overalls and swipes at his brow.

"Hello, Avie."

"No Donnie Dale today?" I ask.

"Nah, his back is acting up."

I lift my eyes upward taking in the clear Carolina blue sky and bright sun.

"It's a warm one today. Are you sure you don't want to take the afternoon off?" I ask.

"No, ma'am. Sabel has me on a strict timeline," he replies.

"Can I at least offer my services? I'm an excellent assistant," I boast.

"I bet you are, but my grandson is pitching in today. He ran over to the house to fetch another sanding blade."

That's good news at least. The old man might be sharp as a tack and strong as an ox, as Sabel claims, but it makes me nervous, watching him through the kitchen window, and the thought of him carrying the large equipment and lumber all by himself is a bit scary.

"Then, how about I whip up a batch of lemonade for the two of you? I just bought a few fresh lemons and mint from the marina market."

He smiles, and the lines around his eyes crinkle. "That'd be lovely," he says.

"Coming right up," I say before heading back to my bags and into the cottage.

I load my wares into the fridge and pantry, then grab a pot from the rack hanging above the kitchen island and set it on the stove.

While the sugar and water create the simple syrup, I take six lemons from the bowl on the counter, slice them in half, and begin juicing them.

When the lemonade is finished, I set the glass pitcher in the refrigerator so it can get nice and cool.

The wonderful aroma of the blossoms from the gardenia bushes out front drifts through the open windows with the breeze, and I note how much different a spring afternoon is here compared to our twenty-first-floor apartment in the city.

Leia is going to love it here.

I find my phone in my purse and click on my playlist. The Bluetooth speaker on the shelf in the living room comes to life, and Norah Jones's soulful voice fills the air.

I love music. All music. One could say I'm a connoisseur of music. From jazz to country, soul, and rock, I am a fan. My father plays many instruments, and my mother is a music teacher in the public school system in Atlanta. They met at a piano bar when they were in college and fell madly in love. I grew up watching them and seeing how much they adored and respected one another. They made it look easy.

I guess that's why I thought my marriage to Conrad would be easy too. I wanted that for Leia so badly.

I shake off the negative thoughts and return to my task. Swaying to the sounds, I muddle fresh mint in the bottom of two tall glasses, then fill them with ice and top it with lemonade.

Placing the glasses on a tray with a plate of chocolate chip cookies I baked last night, I head out the back door and down the stairs, following the sound of the sander.

When I round the side of the cottage, I glimpse a man bent over Sebby's sawhorse. Under the scorching sun, his glistening arms flex with each movement as he toils away. His tanned skin is a testament to the hours he must spend working outdoors. His hair is pulled back into a bun, and I watch as a bead of sweat runs down the length of his muscular back and disappears into the band of his jeans.

Oh my.

When Sebby said his grandson was helping him, I envisioned a cute little boy or a scrawny teen, not this grown man—well grown at that.

"Do you need help with that?" Sebby calls, pulling me from my moment of gawking.

At the sound of his grandfather's voice, the man looks up and over his shoulder in my direction and grins when he catches sight of me.

And my knees give way.

"Whoa there!" Sebby's concerned cry rings out as the tray I was holding goes crashing to the ground.

I jump backward as glass shatters at my feet.

"Are you all right?" Sebby asks as he makes it to me, snapping me back to reality.

"Oh no, I'm sorry. I must have tripped on something," I say as I bend to pick up the tray.

"No, don't. I'll get it. I don't want you to cut yourself," he says as he shoos me away from the mess.

"I'll get a trash bag," I say as the other man approaches.

I turn and run back to the steps leading into the house. Mortified.

Once I'm in the safety of the kitchen, I lean my hands against the cool granite of the island and take a few calming breaths.

Sebastian.

It couldn't be. My imagination just got away from me. There's no way the man I spent an incredible night with in Hawaii all those years ago is standing in the garden of my rental in North Carolina.

He has the same hair. That's all.

I scold myself for being so silly and grab two more glasses. This time, strong mason jars, and I fill them with lemonade. I plate a few more cookies and tuck a trash bag into the pocket of my shorts before heading back out to the scene of the accident.

Sebby is still picking shards from the blades of grass and tossing them into an empty cardboard box, held by his grandson.

"Whoa, let me take those," a deep voice says as he sets the box down on the ground and makes his way to me.

"Thank you," I say as he grabs the jars.

I look up and smile, and then I go still. His bright blue eyes dance with amusement, but not recognition. The same blue eyes that I've seen in my dreams a hundred times. There's no doubt that the man standing before me is Sebastian.

My hot, unforgettable vacation fling.

"My pleasure," he utters.

I swallow hard as I stare up at him.

He grins from ear to ear.

"Are those for us too?" he asks, gesturing to the plate of cookies.

"Oh, yes. I baked a batch for my little girl and thought you guys might enjoy them," I babble.

"Who doesn't like a homemade cookie?" he says as he tucks one of the mason jars under his arm and takes the plate.

He carries it all over to the small green metal table in the garden and sets it down.

Sebby finishes his cleanup efforts, and I take the cardboard box and drop it inside the outdoor waste can on the side of the house.

I spend the rest of the afternoon peering out of the window, watching the two of them work in the garden, like some stalker. My eyes still not believing what they are seeing.

Sebastian is Sabel and Sebby's grandson.

What are the fucking odds?

chapter nine

Sebastian

"So, that's the girl you and Nana rented to for the summer?" I ask as I watch her disappear into the cottage.

"Longer," Gramps answers as he takes a seat across from me at the table.

He grabs a cookie and pops it into his mouth and washes it down with a gulp of lemonade.

"What about her husband? Will he be joining them soon?" I ask as I casually sip from the jar.

Gramps's eyes cut to me. "Nope."

I look back toward the cottage.

Interesting.

"Now, don't go sniffing around your nana's new tenant and pissing her off," he warns.

I turn back to him and grin. "Nana, pissed at me, her precious grandson?"

He shakes his head. "You overestimate your cuteness, son. You aren't the snaggle toothed, towheaded baby she doted on anymore."

I gasp. "I'm still adorable. Just ask her."

He just shakes his head.

"Seriously, I don't know the whole story, but from what I've gathered, listening to your grandmother and Ida Mae's clucking, she was married to some hotshot in New York City, but they divorced last year. She took a job with the sea turtle rescue here in town, and she and their daughter will be here until sometime in November."

"Then what?" I ask.

He shrugs. "I guess they go back to New York."

I sit back against the warm metal of the chair that's been baking in the sun. "November, huh?"

He points his finger at me. "I know that look. You keep your hands to yourself."

I raise my arms in the air in surrender. "You got it, Gramps. Hands off."

We spend the rest of the afternoon building a roof on the hollow oak tree, attaching a door with a tiny window and flower box, and building a step for what is now a fairy house in the middle of the old garden.

Now and then, I glance up to see the curtains sway in the window facing the garden.

Is she watching?

I imagine her big blue eyes trained on me as I work in the sun. Her teeth sink into her plump bottom lip as her gaze slides across my body.

Fuck. I need to get laid.

It's been months since my last relationship sank. If that's what you want to call the three weeks I spent with the granddaughter of Brewster Cartwright.

Brewster is the billionaire CEO of Cartwright Motorsports and Carolina Automotive. The ninety-five-year-old entrepreneur and race promoter, who owns a huge beachfront mansion on the east end of the island, is not my biggest fan.

My friends and I worked for him and his family on their yacht when we were younger, and I admit, I was a bit of a rascal back then. Chasing girls and drinking my paychecks away.

Isn't that what you're supposed to do at that age?

When he found out his precious Alexandria was spending her nights on my boat, he was livid. I tried to tell him that I'd grown up and wasn't the same fuckup I was five years ago, but he wasn't hearing any of it.

All it took was a good dressing-down from him, and Alex was a ghost.

I can't say I blame her. If my grandfather were worth billions and he told me to cut someone loose, I'd be gone too.

Still, that was a damn good three weeks. Little does old Brewster know, but his little Alexandria is a wildcat, and come to find out, my boat wasn't the only one she'd been spending time on.

Nana shows up with a box of painting supplies, and she paints a vine of ivy and tiny pink and purple flowers on the door of the treehouse while Gramps and I secure a small deck off the cedar shake pitched roof and add a set of spiral steps around the back.

"It's adorable," Nana declares once we're finished.

I look over the structure, and it does indeed look like an enchanted tree home for fairies.

"Anything else I can help you guys with before I leave?" I ask.

"Yes. Can you help your grandfather hang the tire swing in the front yard while I get the rug and beanbag chair I bought for this?"

"Rug and chair?" I ask.

"Yes, it will be the perfect place for a little girl to hide away and read or color."

She's really going out of her way to accommodate this tenant and her daughter.

"You always did want a granddaughter of your own, didn't you?" I ask.

She reaches up and pats my cheek.

"I was quite content with you boys, but I must admit, I'm looking forward to some pretty, frilly, girlie things around here for a while."

Nana's hand comes up, and she waves. I glance over my shoulder to see a blonde head step back behind the curtains.

It wasn't my imagination.

I turn back to Nana. "I think I make your new houseguest nervous," I say, and she laughs.

"My goodness, if that head of yours gets any bigger, it won't fit through my front door."

"It's not my fault you and Gramps gave me such outstanding genes," I quip as I wink at her.

She slaps me away, but there is genuine pride in her expression as a blush kisses her cheeks.

"Oh, you devil," she mutters.

Gramps stomps up, hauling a huge tire in a wheelbarrow. A length of rope is wrapped around his shoulder.

My hero.

The man is a machine. In his mid-seventies and still tossing tractor tires around like a twenty-year-old.

"Enough yapping, you two. We're burning daylight," he snaps as he passes us.

Nana halts him and gives him a peck on the cheek.

"Thank you," she says, and his eyes flicker to her and soften.

"You can thank me with shrimp and grits for dinner, woman."

"And a blueberry cobbler for dessert," I add.

She smiles. "You two are so easy to bribe."

She doesn't have to bribe us, and she knows it. We're both pushovers when it comes to her. There's nothing either of us won't do to make her happy.

Gramps mumbles something under his breath and continues to the magnificent oak tree, draped with moss, that stands to the right of the walkway that leads from the street up to the house.

"I'll grab the ladder," I call to him.

chapter Ten

Avie

"MOMMY! MOMMY!"

At the sound of Leia's voice, I sprint from the kitchen to the front door and throw it open.

"Hi, baby," I call as she comes flying up the walkway to where I'm standing on the step.

I wrap my arms around her and lift her into the air.

"I missed you so much," I bellow as I squeeze her tightly.

"I missed you too."

She squirms as I pepper kisses all over her chubby cheeks.

Once I'm all filled back up with baby-girl love and giggles, I look out to see Amiya admiring the Corvette.

"Nice ride. Not sure how you plan to get a car seat into it, but I'm digging the rock-star vibes."

"Yeah, I didn't really think that one through," I grumble.

I called the man at the rental company once I'd already driven away, asking if I could switch vehicles. He told me how to disengage the front passenger airbag and told me that he'd have an SUV available in a couple of weeks if I wanted to trade.

"Well, at least the speed limit in this godforsaken place looks to be twenty-five across the board. You're probably safe," she says as she retrieves Leia's purple suitcase from the back seat of her Mercedes.

She's been less than enthusiastic about our move. When we left New York, she was hoping that we'd land in Atlanta. Truth be told, so was I. I applied for every opening at the Georgia Aquarium, but I was either overqualified or not the right fit. The lead team specialist is interested in me for an aquarist position that is coming available at the end of the year, so I'm keeping my fingers and toes crossed.

"It's not that bad. I think once you have a chance to look around, you might like it here," I say as she gives me a one-armed hug.

"Don't you dare fall in love with Bumfuck, Egypt," she warns.

"Bad word!" Leia scolds.

"Sorry, runt. Auntie Miya is just joking."

No, I'm not, she mouths silently to me.

I lead them inside and down the hallway to the room that Leia will be calling her own for the next six months.

She immediately runs to the big white canopy bed and jumps on it.

"What do you think, kiddo?" I ask.

"It's a princess bed," she squeals.

The moment I saw the bed with the sheer white fabric tied back, I knew she would be ecstatic.

"I have another surprise for you," I say. "Follow me."

She hops off the mattress and sprints over to take hold of my hand. Her brown curls bounce with anticipation.

Amiya rolls her eyes as she falls in behind us. I lead them out the back door and down the steps.

"Whoa," Amiya mutters as she gets sight of the water and pier.

"Nice, right?" I say as I nudge her in the side.

"It's okay, I guess."

I chuckle as we round the side of the house to the white picket fence that surrounds the garden.

Leia gasps as she peeks over the gate to the treehouse.

I go down on one knee and whisper in her ear, "It's your very own fairy garden."

Her eyes go wide. "Do fairies live here?"

I shrug. "I haven't seen any yet, but you know they like to hide from grown-ups, so you'll have to try and find one."

A huge grin spreads across her face as I open the gate, and she skips onto the pebble path and snakes through the flowers and bushes.

"Canopy bed and fairy garden. That kid's never going to want to leave," Amiya points out as we watch Leia explore the wonderland.

"You have to admit, the cottage, the view, it's all pretty spectacular," I say.

"It's all right," she quips.

"There's another interesting fact about Sandcastle Cove," I tell her.

"What's that?"

"The cottage owners' grandson," I say.

"Grandson. Don't tell me he's a prince and he and Leia are going to fall madly in love and live happily ever after."

"He's a little old for Leia."

"Bratty teen?" she asks as she walks over to the wall of hydrangeas and plucks a bloom from the branch. "These are gorgeous. Someone put a lot of work into this space," she muses.

"Amiya, focus," I demand.

She stills at the seriousness of my tone.

"Okay. What?" she asks.

I look over to where Leia is climbing the steps that lead around the back of the tree house and up to the deck.

"Be careful. Hold on to the railing," I call to her before I turn my focus back to my best friend.

"He's here," I say quietly.

"He who?" she asks.

"Sebastian."

"Sebastian who?" she asks.

"What do you mean, Sebastian who?" I bellow, "Sebastian! The Sebastian!"

It takes a moment for it to register, and the minute it does, her head snaps to me.

"What?!" she cries, finally catching on.

Now, I have her attention.

"Yes. He lives here, in Sandcastle Cove. His grandparents are my landlords, for goodness' sake," I reply.

Her eyes go round. "No. No, that's not possible."

"Oh, it is. I mean, what a coincidence, right?" I note.

She shakes her head in disbelief. "Avie, that's not a coincidence. That's … that's … I don't think there's a word in the English language to encompass what that is!"

"Right? I came home yesterday to find him in the garden, helping Sebby build the tree house."

"What did you say when you saw him?" she asks.

"Nothing. I don't think my brain could make coherent sentences at the time. I basically threw a tray of lemonade at them and ran and hid in the house for the rest of the day," I admit.

"I bet."

"He didn't even remember me," I mutter.

She looks at me in disbelief. "He didn't? Are you sure?"

"Positive. He looked me straight in the eye, and there wasn't even a hint of recognition."

She sighs. "In his defense, you were probably one in a million girls he spent a torrid night with while sailing back and forth to

Hawaii on a millionaire's yacht. While he was the only one-night stand you've ever had. Of course you remember him vividly."

"That doesn't make me feel any better," I grumble.

"Divine intervention!" she yells.

"What?"

"That's what it is. There's no other explanation for you coming to this random little North Carolina town and running into the hot fuckboy you took for a spin in Hawaii five years ago," she continues.

"I don't think God's in the business of setting you up to run into your most embarrassing mistake," I state.

"Don't call it that. It was the most significant and carefree moment of your otherwise boring life," she declares.

"I know," I huff.

She steps forward and hooks my neck with her arm. "You really hid in the house all day?"

"And watched him from the window like a creeper."

She roars with laughter. "I do believe this little layover of yours in North Carolina just got a lot more interesting."

That's an understatement.

chapter eleven

Sebastian

WEDNESDAY MORNING, I MAKE MY WAY TO THE MARINA AT the wharf, where our family's fishing boat charter company is located.

Sebby's Charters has been in operation for over fifty years. Gramps and his dad began with one boat and a love of fishing. Now, we have four boats and several employees, including my parents, Gramp's longtime friend Donnie Dale, and my childhood buddies, Anson and Parker. The company is still thriving after all these time and we are booked solid most of the year.

My dad, who married my mom, Milly—Nana and Gramps's daughter—has worked for the company for the last twenty years, but two years ago, he had a seizure while running a charter and was diagnosed with a mild form of epilepsy with non-life-threatening temporal lobe seizures that could be controlled with medication. However, he lost his captain's license and was mandated to the business end of the company, manning a desk instead of a boat.

That's when I came home. It was always the plan for Gramps to retire and Dad to take over with me eventually coming on board after I traveled the world and sowed all my wild oats, but once Dad's condition was uncovered, the plan changed.

Anson and Parker followed me back to Sandcastle Cove, and the three of us joined the team. A decision I don't regret in the least. Working side by side with Gramps has been amazing. I've learned so much from the old man, something I would have missed out on if I'd waited till he was retired to come home.

Besides, there are still plenty of wild oats I can sow right here on my hometown island.

When I first returned, I stayed on the sailboat my parents had given to me as a gift on my twenty-first birthday, but purchased a little beachside cabana last year, just down the road from the condo Anson and Parker share. It's a fixer-upper, and I've been slowly restoring it to its former glory.

Most weekend nights, I still bunk on the boat though, especially during the season when we are taking out full-day charters. It's just me, and it's easier.

Mondays and Tuesdays are our days off, and that's when I dedicate time to the house. As of right now, only one room is finished. My bedroom. It's the most important room in any house—at least in my opinion—so I started there. Now, I've moved on to the kitchen. The second-most-important room.

"Sebastian, did you remember to pick up the new lures?" Gramps calls as I make it to the dock our boats call home.

I raise the box tucked under my arm.

"Good. I'll need those to take the Andersons out today."

"I thought I was taking the Andersons out," I say.

"Bill called and his mother and father decided to join them, so they opted for an inshore charter so Donnie Dale and I will take them out. You and the boys will be giving the other boats a good scrub-down today," he informs me.

Although not sexy, cleaning is an essential part of the job.

"Aye, aye, captain," I say as I give him a quick salute before handing him the box.

Anson and Parker meander on-site, and the three of us get to work.

Wednesdays are our slowest days, especially this early in the year. It affords us time to do all the repairs and maintenance needed. Anson is an excellent boat mechanic, and Parker is a jack-of-all-trades.

We make a great team and crew.

The boats are rinsed daily, and the motors are flushed with fresh water after every ocean excursion, but today, we'll be pulling out the big guns.

Parker drags over the wheeled power washer from the office as I raise the first boat out of the water. The pressure will help clean stubborn floors, gunwales, and console grime after Anson and I scrub them down with soapy water.

Parker sets to start the exterior, motor, and trailer while we work on the interior.

Once everything is clean, we work together to apply the fiberglass wax to seal the surface and prevent it from becoming ingrained with and damaged by surface dirt.

One by one, we knock out the fleet.

Around one, Nana shows up with a picnic basket and a little girl who has curly brown hair and the most angelic face I've ever seen.

"Well, who do we have here?" I ask as I take the basket and lift it aboard the boat.

"This is Leia. She is our tenant's daughter. She's spending the afternoon with me while her mother is down at the turtle hospital. Leia, this is my grandson, Sebastian. He works on the boats with Sebby," Nana explains.

"Nice to meet you, Bastian," a sweet, melodic voice calls.

I grin down at the adorable child. "Nice to meet you," I say before returning my attention to my grandmother. "You taking on a new career in babysitting, Nana?" I ask.

"I'm not a baby!" the little girl barks, that sweet voice going up a few octaves.

I snap my eyes to hers and quirk an eyebrow. "You're not?"

She shakes her head, and the curls bounce like tiny springs.

"My apologies, ma'am," I say before returning my questioning gaze to Nana.

"Ida Mae and I offered to keep Leia here for her mother a few days a week until she's able to find a suitable day care. She had signed her up for Little Miss Sunshine at the end of the Westside Bridge, but Ida Mae and I have heard a few troubling things about that place."

Sure they have.

"Thank goodness she had you and Ida Mae to save the day," I say with a wink.

"Are you a good captain, like Cap'n Crunch, or a bad captain, like Captain Hook?" Leia asks me.

The question throws me off.

"Crunch or Hook? That's an odd duo," I say.

"They aren't a duo. They're not even friends," she says.

I laugh out loud.

Her confused eyes narrow on me.

"What's so funny?"

"Let me ask you a question. Are you a good princess, like Princess Leia?"

"Nope. I'm a mighty warrior, like General Leia," she declares.

"She told you," Anson says as he walks past us.

"That's very cool."

"Well?" Leia asks impatiently.

"Well?" I ask.

She huffs. "Are you good or bad?"

"I'm a good captain, like Cap'n Crunch," I assure her.

She smiles, and two dimples pop out from her chubby cheeks. "Can I come on your boat?"

"Permission to come aboard granted," I say as I move to the side.

She lets go of Nana's hand and prances up the walk. Then, she looks back at me and extends her tiny hand.

I take it and help her down onto the deck.

Our company mascot—my parents' golden retriever pup—scurries over to say hello to the newest guest.

"It's a puppy!" Leia squeals.

"That's Minnow. He's my co-captain. He helps me sail the boat."

She giggles as the pup pounces up and down, licking her face.

"I think he likes you," I say.

"He's so cute," she says as Minnow knocks her over onto her bottom.

I pick the puppy up by its scruff, and it wiggles, trying to get back to her.

"Settle," I command, and he instantly calms.

I set him on the bench in the back of the boat and tell him to stay before turning back to our visitor.

"Wow, this is a big one," she says as she runs over to the wheel, where Parker is seated. "Do you have a pirate ship too?"

"A pirate ship? No. Cap'n Crunch doesn't own a pirate ship. I do have a sailboat though," I reply.

"Can you take me on the sailboat?"

She's an adventurous little thing.

"Maybe one day."

"Today is one day," she responds.

Parker chuckles. "She's got you there."

Nana comes aboard and begins to unload wrapped sandwiches from the picnic basket I set on the table.

"How about we eat and then discuss boat rides?" she suggests.

Leia climbs up onto the cushioned bench by the table and settles with her knees underneath her.

"Are there sharks in the water?" she asks as she removes the brown paper from a chicken salad sandwich and takes a huge bite.

"Not this close to the pier," I answer.

"What about mermaids?"

I bend down and whisper, "I've seen a couple, but it's a secret, and we aren't supposed to talk about it."

Her eyes go wide. "Really? I want to be a mermaid when I grow up."

I raise my eyebrows. "I thought you wanted to be a fairy princess?"

Her head tilts to the side. "Who told you?" she asks.

"Nana did. When I was building the fairy house in the garden at your cottage."

"You built it?" she asks.

"I helped."

"Well, I can be a princess *and* a mermaid."

"Both?"

She shrugs. "Yep, just like Ariel," she says around a mouthful of sandwich.

"A fairy princess mermaid?"

"Sure. That way, I can live under the sea or fly in the air and marry a prince and rule the kingdom."

I nod as I open a bag of barbeque chips onto a paper towel and take a bite. "Good plan."

"I know," she says as she steals a potato chip off my napkin.

"Hey," I say as I tickle her side.

She starts giggling, and Nana tells us both to behave and eat our lunch.

"Yes, ma'am," we say in unison.

chapter twelve

Avie

I SPENT THE AFTERNOON OBSERVING A FEEDING DEMONSTRATION AT the turtle hospital, which hosted a group of children from the local middle school. I wanted to introduce myself to the other employees and get a lay of the land ahead of my first day on the job.

The staff is wonderful. Very welcoming and knowledgeable.

After the presentation, Glenna—an older, soft-spoken woman with a kind smile, who has been at the rehab center for over a decade—gave me a tour of the hospital and introduced me to the current patients. One of whom is Otis, an estimated sixty-year-old green sea turtle, who was caught in a fishing net and suffered from a mangled flipper, which the doctor had to amputate. He's now being rehabbed, and once he learns to swim again, he will hopefully be able to be returned to the ocean.

I text Sabel once I am back in my car, and she replies that she and Leia went down to the marina to have a late lunch with Sebby, but he was on an unplanned charter, so they decided to stick around and enjoy the weather by the water. I tell her that I'll come to them, and I head that way.

The salty tang of the sea fills the air, and the late-day sun warms my cheeks as I make my way up the creaking steps that lead to the wooden docks.

The wharf is a whirl of activity this evening. Folks are standing in line at the Boathouse Restaurant, waiting for seats. The hum of a band organ floats up from the slowly spinning carousel, and announcements for chartered boat parties blast over the speakers.

In the distance, I catch the peal of giggles, mingling with the squawking of seagulls and the low purr of boat engines.

I follow the sound of Leia's laughter toward the bustling marina until I spy her sweet brown curls bobbing in the wind as she chases the birds across the pier. She is wearing a small yellow life vest over her blue sundress.

Sabel is on a bench close by, bellowing for Leia to slow down and be careful.

I sneak up on her, grab her waist, and hoist her into the air.

"Mommy! Did you see the gulls? Aren't they cool?"

"I saw someone aggravating the seagulls," I reply.

Sabel stands and walks over to us.

"How was your afternoon, dear?" she asks.

"It was great. Thank you for watching her for me. I hope she wasn't too much trouble."

"No trouble at all." She asks Leia, "We had a great time together, didn't we?"

"The best! I met Cap'n Crunch," Leia yells.

I hear chuckling, and my attention is drawn to a fishing boat docked to our right.

"That'd be me."

Sebastian's voice causes my legs to go weak again, and I shakily set Leia on her feet.

"Mommy, come look! We caught a fish," Leia calls as she runs toward the boat, Sabel on her heels.

"You did?"

She looks back at me and nods as Sabel begins introductions.

"Avie, you remember Sebby and Donnie Dale. This is Anson and

Parker, who work for Sebby, and you met our grandson, Sebastian," she says as she pats the back of the man leaning against the side of the boat.

He stands and throws his hand up to greet me.

A huge smile spreads across his face as his sea blue eyes meet mine. "It's nice to meet you. Again."

"You too," I choke out.

There's no recognition in his expression, but Anson comes up behind him, and his eyes squint in my direction.

"What did you say your name was?" he asks.

"Avie. Avie Sullivan," I reply.

His eyes go wide, and a grin spreads from ear to ear.

"Hawaiian Barbie!" he cries.

That's when Sebastian's head whips around, and his gaze focuses on me.

"Avie?" he utters.

"Yeah," is all I manage to say.

Anson and Parker hop down from the vessel and over to me.

"Wow, that's crazy. What brings you to Sandcastle Cove?" Parker asks.

"Work actually," I reply.

"Fantastic. Is Amiya with you?" Anson says.

"No, she's in Atlanta, but she's coming to stay with us for two weeks in July."

He even remembers my friend's name. Brownie points for Anson.

He looks back to Sabel, who is standing on the deck between Sebby and Sebastian, and explains, "We met Avie and her friend in Hawaii." He asks me, "What was it, like, six, seven years ago?"

"Five," I answer.

Sabel brings her eyes to me. "Really?"

I nod. "I would have said something, but when I met Sebastian the other day, I wasn't quite sure if he was the same Sebastian."

That sounded lame, even to me.

My gaze flutters up to him, and he is still staring at me.

"Your hair is lighter and longer," is all he says.

I reach up and run my fingers through the strands that are flying around in the breeze. "Is it?"

"Yeah, and you're ..." He doesn't finish the thought aloud as his eyes skim down my body.

"You're different too," I point out.

And he is. His shoulders are broader, and his face is harder somehow. Less carefree maybe. A smattering of dark hair covers his square jaw. It ages him, but I like it.

Like a fine wine.

The mature, sexy, rugged look. It suits him.

"Isn't this an interesting development?" Sabel declares as she looks at Sebby.

"Downright kismet," he agrees.

"Come on, Mommy," Leia calls.

I reluctantly walk up the pier, and Sebby helps me onto the deck.

I follow Leia over to a cooler at the back of the boat, and she opens the lid.

Inside is a largemouth bass.

"Wow, you caught that?" I ask.

"Bastian caught it, and I helped him reel it in," she says as she leans over the edge.

"That's amazing, baby. I'm proud of you."

"He's gonna get me a rod my size and teach me how to do it all by myself," she informs me.

I look over my shoulder to Sebastian, who is watching us from the front of the boat.

"He is, huh?"

"Yeah, he promised."

"That's very nice of him," I say without breaking eye contact with him.

I stand and reach my hand out to her. "Come on. You've had a big day. We need to get you home and feed you dinner," I say.

"Ah, do we have to?" she whines, a clear indication that she's tired.

"Yes, we do. Now, let's go and thank everyone for being so nice today."

She takes my outstretched hand and stomps over to the crowd.

"Leia," I prompt.

"Thank you," she mumbles quietly. Her bottom lip protruding.

Sebastian goes down to a knee and looks her in the eyes. "Now, that's not a very fairy princess mermaid attitude," he says as he taps the tip of her nose.

She grunts, and it makes him chuckle as he stands back up.

"I'm sorry. She gets grumpy when she's tired," I explain.

He shrugs. "So do I."

An awkward silence grows between us before Sabel interrupts.

"I'll go with you guys since her car seat is in my vehicle. How does that sound?"

"Yes!" Leia wails.

Sabel turns and kisses Sebby as I remove the life vest from Leia and hand it to Sebastian.

"Avie Sullivan," he mutters as he takes it from my hand.

"Sebastian Hollister?"

"Harraway," he corrects.

"Sebastian Harraway," I repeat.

"It's good to see you again," he says, and my stomach does a little flip.

"You too."

"Mommy," Leia calls as Sabel steps off the deck onto the pier.

"Right, let's go," I say as I pick her up and rest her on my hip.

Sebby takes my other arm and helps us down, and we follow Sabel to the parking lot.

chapter thirteen

Sebastian

"You can stop eye-fucking her now," Anson says, and my attention moves from the three of them walking away to him.

I toss the small yellow life jacket onto his head. "Shut up, dip-shit. My grandfather is standing right here."

Anson snickers. "He saw it too."

Gramps grunts and shakes his head at us before hopping out of the boat and heading for the office.

"I can't believe you didn't tell us she was here," Parker says.

"I had no idea."

He stops mopping and looks up at me. "You seriously didn't recognize her?" he asks.

"That's what happens when you get so much ass. You can't keep up with it," Anson teases.

Parker turns to him. "Lucky for you, that's not a problem you'll ever have."

I drown out their bickering as I berate myself for not recognizing the girl I spent one hell of a night with all those years ago. I'm sure she thinks I'm an asshole.

And she'd be right.

But she does look different. Her hair is longer, and her lean body has gained some beautiful curves that weren't there before.

"Earth to Sebastian." Parker brings my attention back to him as he snaps his fingers in my face.

I push him away. "What?"

"Are we going out tonight?" he asks.

Wednesday night is two-dollar draft night at Whiskey Joe's. The three of us usually head straight there after work.

"Of course."

"Then, let's get this shit done and get out of here," Parker exclaims.

We walk into Whiskey Joe's, and Anson grabs a table near the stage while Parker and I make our way to the bar.

Audrey, a sultry redhead, slides up to the old scarred bar. She leans over it in a way that makes her voluptuous breasts, which are currently peeking out of her low-cut tank top, spill over to give us a nice show.

"Hey, Sebastian. I was beginning to think you guys weren't gonna show up tonight," she purrs.

I place my elbows on the mahogany wood and lick my lips as my eyes go straight to the spot she wants them to.

"Now, you know we're here every Wednesday," I say.

Parker's throat clears behind me, and her eyes lift to him.

"What can I get you guys?" she asks.

Parker slaps a hundred-dollar bill on the bar. "Three drafts. Keep 'em coming," he grunts.

She stands up and reaches for three glasses and places them under the taps to the left.

"Someone is grumpy," she mutters under her breath.

Once she's taken the money and handed over our order, Parker walks away.

"Thanks, Audrey. We're at the table by the stage," I inform her.

"Got it. I'll have Heather bring your next round in about thirty."

One of the local country bands greets the crowd to a round of thundering applause.

"I have to hit the head," Parker says as he kicks his chair back and stands.

When he's out of earshot, I look at Anson.

"What crawled up his ass?" I ask.

Anson chuckles as he takes a sip of his beer. "Dude, you are so fucking blind sometimes. He has a thing for Audrey. Has since high school," he explains.

My brows crease. "So, his strategy is to be a dick to her?"

Anson shakes his head. "Yeah, when she pulls her tits out and practically crawls over the bar to get to your lap, the dick comes out."

"That's just what she does. She's a bartender. Those tits get her bigger tips," I state.

"I know that, and you know that, but all he sees is her batting her eyes at you and you licking your lips like you're about to take her up on what she's offering you on a silver platter. And she is, offering it up."

He's wrong. Audrey turned down a drunken invite to the boat months ago. She and Alex are friends, and even if she were interested in me, she wouldn't cross that line.

I grasp the glass in front of me and down the contents as Parker rejoins us.

"Heather looks like she's bogged down. Park, why don't you go grab our next round from Audrey?" I suggest.

He looks over his shoulder at the bar. "Probably get them quicker if you go."

I shake my head and stand. "I got my eye on a brunette in a pair of tiny jean shorts. I'm going to ask her to dance before someone else does," I tell him.

"Really? Which one?" Parker asks as he looks around the dance floor.

I point to the girl who is currently dancing with another girl. Both are staring our way.

"Nice," he says.

I take off in their direction.

"Yep, now, go get our beers," I call.

I spin the two giggly girls around the dance floor a few times before returning to our table.

"Shot down?" Parker asks.

"They're eighteen years old, here on spring break. That's just trouble. I'm not touching that," I reply.

"Damn, every year, the college girls look older," he mumbles.

That's the damn truth.

Anson chuckles.

"What?" Parker asks.

"Eighteen. Perfectly legal. And I'm not buying that you suddenly have some gentlemanly conscience. I think he still has another college girl on his mind."

I quirk an eyebrow at him. "What the fuck are you talking about? What other college girl?"

"Avie," he says.

"Avie is not a college girl," I say.

"Not anymore, but she was when we met her. And the way

you were staring at her this evening, I'd say you still have a hard-on for her."

"You're such a prick—you know that?" I spit.

He grins. "It's part of my charm."

Heather appears between Parker and me. "Charm? You, Anson Leggett? That's a stretch."

He sits up straight, and his grin widens. "You wound me," he tells her.

She rolls her eyes. "Can I get you guys anything?"

"Food?" I ask them.

"Yes. Nachos and a double order of buffalo wings. Extra blue cheese," Anson says.

"Sounds good to me," Parker agrees.

We spend the rest of the evening choking down cheap beer and artery-clogging bar snacks. Parker and I leave around midnight while Anson sticks around, waiting for Heather's shift to end.

"You good to drive?" Parker asks as we climb into my Bronco.

"Yep. Cut myself off at three an hour and a half ago."

I put the key in the ignition and look over at him as he clicks his seat belt in place.

"You sure you don't want to stay with Anson and wait for Audrey?" I ask.

"Fuck no," he quips.

"Why not?"

He cuts his eyes to me. "She's not interested."

"You never know till you ask," I advise.

"Thanks, Dad, but I'm not the one she throws herself at."

"Park, she's just flirting because I flirt with her like I flirt with everyone. She doesn't take it seriously, and neither do I. If you want the woman, you have to make it clear to her."

He leans back into the seat.

Maybe next Wednesday, then.

I drop him off at the condo, and instead of heading back to the marina, I pull into the beach house.

As I walk up the steps that lead to the ocean-facing deck, I make a note to replace the wood on the first three.

I unlock the door and walk into the living room, filled with plastic-covered furniture, coated with a layer of sawdust, and into the kitchen, where the cabinets have been removed and the frame for the new island stands. Plucking a beer from the fridge, I make my way to the bedroom and the big king-size bed, remove my shoes, and climb on.

What a day.

I still can't believe that the girl who left me high and dry in Honolulu all those years ago is living in my grandparents' cottage.

What are the fucking odds?

My mind drifts back to that night.

Her legs wrap around me, and she circles her hips, moving more urgently, seeking the release her body wants so badly.

I increase my thrusts, giving her what she wants, when her legs—those incredible legs—tense around me, and she begins to shudder.

"Look at me, Avie," I command.

Her head snaps up, and I watch as she loses the battle and shatters around me.

Her cries fill the cabin and echo against the walls as her pussy tightens around me.

I stiffen atop her, and my cry mingles with hers as she milks my orgasm from me.

I put the bottle on the nightstand beside the bed, stand, and strip on my way into the bathroom.

Once I'm under the hot spray of the shower, I plant a hand on the wall and fist my rock-hard cock with the other.

I fuck my hand as I envision the wild, sexy abandon in her eyes that night. I get lost in the memory of her sweat-slick skin gliding against mine and the sound of her cries of pleasure until a stream of hot, thick cum splashes on the tiles, and I sag against my arm to catch my breath.

Fuck, I'm in trouble.

chapter fourteen

Avie

THE WEEKEND WAS A BLUR.

Leia and I spent Saturday on the beach, building sandcastles and swimming in the surf until she was so exhausted that she couldn't keep her eyes open.

Sunday, we rode from one end of the island to the other on the golf cart, which she thought was the best thing since sliced bread.

Every resident of Sandcastle Cove gave their horn a toot and waved as we passed them. Leia excitedly yelled her hello to them all.

We have one more week to explore before I'll be required to be at the rehab center four days a week. I've tried desperately to find a suitable day care for Leia, but they are all full. She has been added to two waiting lists so far, but the prospects are getting dim.

Sabel and Ida Mae promised me that they didn't mind keeping her, but when I offered to pay, they both refused. As kind as the gesture is, I feel like I'm taking advantage of them.

"Oh, don't be silly. We enjoy the company. It's been a long time since either of us has had the pitter-patter of little feet around the house," Sabel assured me, and I relented. What other choice did I have?

Now, it's Monday afternoon, and I'm enjoying the cove, sunbathing in my bikini on the deck of the boat dock while Leia runs amok in the garden.

I pull my hair up in a messy knot on top of my head and slather on Sun Bum tanning lotion before lying back on the beach towel I have sprawled over the wooden planks. Closing my eyes, I listen to the gentle lapping of the water, mingled with the sound of Leia's giggles and chatter. Relishing in the peace of it all until the hum of a motor invades the moment.

I sit up and bring my hand to shade my eyes from the sunlight.

A small runabout boat with a wood-paneling exterior and two captain's chairs with a cream leather bench pulls up to the dock.

Sebastian is behind the wheel.

I watch as he turns off the ignition and ties the boat into place.

He's wearing a pair of low-slung swim trunks and a white T-shirt that pulls tight across his shoulders as he wrangles the rope. His hair is tied back, and his eyes are covered by a pair of aviator sunglasses.

Once the boat is secure, he walks over to me and lifts his shades so I'm able to see his eyes as they sweep over me.

"Hi, Avie Sullivan," he greets.

"Hi yourself, Sebastian Harraway."

"I remember that bikini," he says, heat in his gaze caressing my skin like a physical touch.

I look down at the white swimsuit. It's my favorite, and I've had it for years.

"And what a great fucking memory it is," he grits out.

My eyes shoot back up to him, and all of a sudden, the air feels too thick, and I can't seem to get any into my lungs.

He grins at my reaction.

I open my mouth to offer a retort when Leia comes pouncing down the stepping stone path.

"Bastian!"

His attention snaps to her. "Hey, little one. What do you have there?" he asks.

She runs up to him, a tangle of colorful blooms clutched in her fist.

"It's flowers for Mommy," she announces.

"Very nice," he says as he lifts her off her feet and rests her on his hip.

She looks over at his boat. "Where's Minnow?" she asks.

"He's with my mom and dad."

Her brows furrow. "I thought he was your co-captain."

He chuckles. "Boy, you don't forget a thing, do you?" he asks.

"Mommy says I'm the best remember-er," she tells him proudly.

"Yep," I sigh.

"I promise I'll bring him next time," he says.

"Never forgets anything," I sing and laugh, as he's obviously unskilled at handling four-year-olds.

"Did you come to play with us?" she asks him.

"Actually, I came to play with Sebby. He and I are going to spread some pebble stones around the firepit for Nana," he replies.

"Why?" she asks.

"Because she likes the way they look and it's less grass for Gramps to have to cut in the summer," he explains.

"Oh," she says like that made perfect sense to her.

He places her back on her feet. "Tell you what though. You and your mom can come over later, and we'll light a fire and roast some marshmallows if you want."

She turns to me. "Can we, Mommy? Pretty please!"

"Only if Sebby and Sabel say it's okay," I tell her.

She looks back at Sebastian.

"You tell them that Mommy said it's okay if they say it's okay."

The corner of his mouth lifts. "I'll do that."

"Thanks," she says before handing me the now-smashed and wilting flowers before skipping back off toward the garden.

"I'd better get to it. See you in a bit. You should wear that," he says as his eyes skim me again and he walks past.

I roll my eyes.

"Make sure your grandparents want company before you invite us next time," I call after him.

I flip back down on the towel.

So much for relaxing.

Sabel calls while I'm feeding Leia dinner and tells us to come over for the fire and marshmallow roast as soon as we're ready.

I change into a sundress and send Leia to find her flip-flops when I hear a car pull into the drive.

Pulling open the door to investigate, I'm surprised when I see Amiya's silver Mercedes.

"What are you doing here?"

"Not exactly the greeting I was hoping for. Aren't you happy to see me?" she asks as she exits the car.

"Of course I am. I'm just surprised. You've only been gone a little over a week," I say.

"Like I'm gonna miss a moment of this sexy saga you have playing out here in paradise. I told my boss I was going to be working remotely this week," she says as she reaches into the back seat and pulls out a suitcase.

"Aunt Miya," Leia squeals as she comes skidding out of the door and down the steps.

"LeLe!" Amiya shouts as she goes to a knee and opens her arms.

Leia runs full throttle into her.

Amiya closes her into a tight hug.

"Now, that's the way you greet someone," she calls over Leia's shoulder.

I laugh. "Next time, I promise."

She lets Leia go and stands and grabs the handle of her bag.

"We're going to eat mellows," Leia exclaims.

"You are?"

Leia nods. "Bastian is making them in the backyard."

Amiya looks at me. "Oh, is he now?"

"Not now. In a minute, when we get there. You can come too," Leia says.

"Well, thank you. I'd love to go eat mellows with Bastian," Amiya coos as she passes me and steps into the cottage.

"You're gonna have to share a canopy bed with a squirming four-year-old," I call after her.

"I've shared a bed with worse," she retorts.

chapter fifteen

Sebastian

Parker and Anson showed up to help Gramps and me finish our project, but Nana put them to work, assembling the new Adirondack chairs she'd bought for the new firepit with a promise of fried chicken and squash casserole for dinner.

After we feed our faces, the three of us haul wood from under the deck and stack it in the wrought iron rack by the patio while Gramps gets a fire going.

Nana arranges the chairs by color and places the last one just as the fence gate opens, and Avie, Leia, and her friend from Hawaii, Amiya, come walking through.

Leia has two bags of extra-large marshmallows tucked in her arms.

"Well, well, look what the cat dragged in," Anson says as they make it to us.

"Hi, boys. Long time no see," Amiya quips as she hugs Parker.

"Sebby, Sabel, this is my best friend, Amiya. She surprised us with a visit this evening," Avie introduces.

"I hope it's okay if I join you," Amiya says.

"Of course. The more, the merrier," Nana says as she gestures for them to take a seat.

Leia walks over to me and lifts her bags. "We found great big marshmallows," she squeals.

"I see that. Good job, kid."

I take the bags from her and extend my knuckles, and she gives me a fist bump.

Nice.

"And I found wine," Amiya says as she waves a bottle of red in the air.

I run inside to gather the metal skewers Nana has to roast marshmallows or weenies over an open fire and a wine bottle opener for the girls. Just as I'm about to exit, Avie walks in.

"Sabel sent me in for Solo cups," she says.

"Yeah, should be in the cupboard above the sink," I tell her.

She slides past me, and I wait for her to find them.

Once she has them, I open the door and hold it for her.

"Thanks," she says, a soft smile on her lips.

"You're welcome."

We join the others, and Leia sits on Nana's lap as she helps her spear one of the marshmallows with a skewer and holds it in the dancing flames.

"So, you're out of the yacht-piloting business?" Amiya asks.

"Until I win the lottery and buy my own," I answer.

"Or just convinces one of his sugar mamas to buy one for him," Anson quips.

"Sugar mama?" Amiya asks. lifting an eyebrow in my direction.

"Don't listen to him."

"Sugar *mamas*," Anson stresses.

"Shut up, dipshit," I yell as I throw a marshmallow at his head.

"Plural, huh?" Amiya quips.

Anson catches the sticky ball and tosses it aside. "Yep. The island fills up with them every summer. Wealthy women looking for a hot and heavy vacation affair," he explains.

"Nice," Avie murmurs.

My eyes cut to her. "You date one forty-something divorcée, and you never hear the end of it," I mutter as I roll my eyes and grin.

"She bought him a Jet Ski," Anson states.

"Really?" Amiya notes.

"It was a birthday gift," I justify.

Anson chuckles. "Just sayin', all my girlfriend got me for my birthday was a card and a cake."

"Like you have a girlfriend," I toss back.

I turn my attention to Avie. "I don't hook up with older divorcées every summer."

"That's true. It was a few years ago, but what a summer," Anson bellows.

"You rascals need to change the subject," Nana scolds as she points down at Leia.

"Sorry, Nana," Anson mumbles.

"What's a rascal?" Leia asks as she looks up at her.

"A very naughty boy," Nana replies.

Leia nods. "Boys are naughty rascals."

We all burst into laughter, but my focus shifts back to Avie, who's lost in her red plastic cup filled with wine.

Fucking Anson.

"What about you, Avie? Didn't you give up the big job and expense account in the city to watch turtle nests on a small coastal island in North Carolina?" I ask.

She shrugs. "Yeah, maybe. I mean, my job in New York wasn't that glamorous. It was mostly research, writing papers for grants, and things like that. But I did have a nice, big corner office with a view of Uptown."

I lean forward so I hear her better over the crackle of the fire.

"So, tell me, why would you walk away from that?" I'm genuinely curious.

"Honestly, I just needed a change. I chose to study marine science because I love the ocean and the animals that call it home. I don't mind research, but I want to be hands-on. To have a chance to work with the animals, the coral, and the reefs, not just for them. And I want Leia to experience something other than the loud, rushed city. She should be spending her days playing in gardens and chasing fireflies, like I did when I was a kid, because before I know it, she's going to be in kindergarten and spending the next twelve years going to school and coming home to hours of homework and extracurricular activities. Now's the time for her world to be filled with magic."

"You picked a good place, then. There's nothing like the magic of Sandcastle Cove," Nana says.

Avie looks at her. "I'm beginning to see that."

"I can carry her," Avie says as we make our way across the low-lit street.

A sleeping Leia is cradled in my arms.

"I'm sure you can, but you're three Solo cups in," I remind her.

She hiccups. "I'm not drunk," she insists.

"I didn't say you were."

We left to tuck the little girl in bed as Nana and Amiya were raiding the dinner leftovers and heating plates of chicken for everyone. Nana sent Parker and Gramps on a wine run, and Anson is keeping an eye on the fire so it doesn't go out.

Avie opens the door, and I walk inside the cottage.

"This way," she whispers as she tiptoes down the hallway. "We'll put her in my room," she says as she opens the door on the left.

I carefully place the sleeping girl in the middle of the king-size bed, and she curls into a ball against the pillows. Avie crawls up to tightly tuck the covers around her. Then, she places a light kiss on her forehead.

"Sweet dreams, baby girl," she murmurs before we back out quietly.

Once we're in the hallway, she pulls the door shut.

"You hungry?" I ask as I follow her.

She stops and presses her back against the wall. "I think I should stay," she says.

"I thought you wanted fried chicken?"

"I do, but I don't feel comfortable with leaving Leia. I know she's asleep, and it's just across the street, but what if she wakes up and needs me and I'm not here?"

"You want me to bring you a plate?" I ask.

She blinks up at me from beneath her long lashes.

"Amiya can bring me one," she says.

I lean into her and brush a loose strand of hair from her face, resting my hand on the side of her throat.

"Yeah, but do you want me to bring it to you?" I ask.

I take a step closer, and her breath hitches, drawing my eyes to her chest as it rises and falls.

My hand slides down, and my thumb strokes the pulse point just below her ear.

Her teeth sink into her bottom lip, and her eyes flutter shut.

"Avie?"

She looks back up at me.

"What do you want?" I ask.

"I ..." She presses into me and tilts her head back, and just as I'm about to dip down and take her mouth with mine, the front door flies open, and Amiya rounds the corner.

"Sabel sent me with a doggie bag—oops," she gasps as she catches sight of us.

I groan.

"Um, I'll just be in the kitchen," Amiya mutters as she turns around.

I look back at Avie, and I know the moment has passed.

"I should probably go eat something," she says as she stares after her friend.

And it looks like I'll be spending another night with nothing but the company of my hand in the shower.

chapter sixteen

Avie

"SAY CHEESE," AMIYA SAYS AS SHE SHOVES HER PHONE IN MY face and snaps a photo.

"What are you doing?" I ask as I shove her away.

She plops down on the outdoor couch in front of her laptop that's perched on the coffee table.

"Setting you up with a dating profile online," she replies.

"Oh, no, you're not."

"I am."

I lunge for her laptop, but she's faster than me and grabs hold of it.

"You said you were willing to try one if I did," she reminds me.

"I said that to appease you. I wasn't serious."

"Well, I was, and I met a couple of really great guys since I signed up. Now, what do you want your profile to say?"

I know she isn't going to let this go, so I just go with it.

"I don't know. Something simple and honest," I say.

Amiya's mouth twists as she thinks.

"Got it! *Frumpy, tired single mother seeks attentive, average-looking man who likes sassy four-year-olds and awkwardly codependent best friends who never go away,*" she states as she begins to type.

"Amiya!"

"There. It's simple and honest," she says as she clicks away.

I look down at myself in my baggy sage-green sweatpants and white tank, then back to her. "You think I'm frumpy?"

"Terribly so," she replies.

I slide my eyes over to Leia, who is playing on the rug.

"What about you, squirt?" I ask.

She glances up from her Legos and squints at me. "You should wear more sparkles," she states matter-of-factly.

My mouth falls open, and I crouch down to tickle her.

"*Et tu, Brute*?"

Leia starts squirming, scattering the foot-piercing plastic pieces across the porch.

"What's a brutrey?" she asks through giggles.

"It's a traitor," I bellow.

"I'm not a trailer," she wails.

"Not trailer. Traitor. You're supposed to be on my side."

"I am. I am," she wheezes.

Amiya shuts the laptop and looks at me as I roll over Leia and lie down on the soft shag.

"You could skip the bullshit and just email your profile straight to Sebastian," she suggests.

I look at Leia, who is lost in her play again.

"Little ears," I stress.

"Sorry. You can skip the crap and send your profile straight to Hawaiian hottie," she rephrases.

I push myself up and join her on the couch.

"I'm not interested in pursuing anything with him."

"Hmm, didn't look that way when I walked in on the two of you in the hallway last night," she muses.

"Nothing was going on," I protest.

"Please. You could cut the sexual tension with a knife. I got high on the pheromones you two were emitting. They were like gasoline fumes about to ignite and burn the house down."

"You're worse than a man—you know that?"

She grins. "You mean, *better* than a man."

"I can't believe you made plans with them last night," I say as we climb out of the golf cart.

Sebastian, Anson, and Parker are waiting for us in the parking lot.

"They offered to take us out. What was I supposed to say? Besides, I think Anson is just as interested in watching you and Sebastian combust as I am," Amiya teases.

Great.

When we make it to the boys, they guide us up the ramp to the entrance to the Beacon Seafood Buffet Restaurant.

"I hope you girls are ready to eat your weight in fried seafood," Sebastian states.

"Leia loves crab legs," I say.

"Really? So do I. They're my favorite," he tells Leia.

"I bet I'll eat more than you," she challenges.

He gives her a pacifying grin.

"No way. You're just a little girl," he replies.

"I bet you ice cream," she declares confidently as she extends her hand.

He eyes her suspiciously. "Why do I feel like I'm being hustled?"

I laugh as he takes her fingers into his and shakes.

Leia grins and then skips off toward the front door of the restaurant.

"Because you are, sucker," Amiya whispers as we breeze past him.

The hostess leads us to a high-top table on the glassed-in deck at the back of the restaurant.

The waitress brings us each a glass of water, and Leia asks for Sprite.

"And we don't need these." Anson hands her back the stack of menus the hostess left on the table with our wrapped silverware. "We'll all be having the buffet, and we'll need crab legs crackers and mallets."

"And a bowl of melted butter. Not a little ketchup bowl. A big one, with Old Bay sprinkled on top, and a lobster bib, please," Leia requests.

Sebastian looks at her and quirks an eyebrow. "I like your style, kid."

Amiya stays with Leia while I follow the boys over to the buffet. I grab two plates from the stack, walk straight to the crab legs station, and pile them both high.

"You have to try the lobster mac, clam chowder, and salmon risotto," Parker says as he lifts the ladle from a stainless steel pot and fills a bowl with thick, creamy soup.

"I will. I'm just making Leia's plates first," I say.

His eyes go wide. "Both of those are for her?" His chin jerks toward the two mounds of crab legs that I can barely see over.

"Oh, yeah," I reply.

He bursts out laughing.

I return to the table, and the waitress has brought Leia a Styrofoam cup of Sprite. I unwrap a straw for her and slide the beverage in front of her. Then, I set the hot bowl of butter on a saucer and place it to her right, tie the plastic bib around her neck, and give her one of the crackers.

"Thank you, Mommy," she says as she comes up on her knees so she can better reach the pile of delicious crustaceans.

The boys arrive back with their plates.

Sebastian has a stack of legs, but he also has fried oysters, scallops, peel-and-eat shrimp, mac 'n' cheese, coleslaw, and a handful of hush puppies.

Amiya eyes his feast. "That's a lot of food there, big boy."

"I have a big appetite."

"Hope you'll have room for ice cream," she mutters.

We leave Leia with them, and Amiya and I go grab an assortment of deep-fried delicacies for ourselves.

By the time we make it back to our seats, Leia has destroyed one of the plates in front of her.

All three of the men are staring at her in a mix of admiration and disbelief as she continues to crack and rip apart the crab legs with ease. Snatching the sweet meat from its shell and using her fingers to dip it into the butter and slurp it between her lips.

"Ready for another round, I see," Amiya says as she sets her plate down and returns to the crab legs station.

For the next hour and a half, we keep the waitress busy, removing platters of empty shells and replacing the bowls of butter as Sebastian goes head-to-head with my little one.

She's faster and more efficient at gleaning the meat from its casing and finishes her fourth plate before he has made it through his third.

"How's that chowder?" Parker asks me when he catches me practically licking the bowl.

"Hated it," I state.

He chuckles.

My phone chimes, and I ignore it, but Amiya wipes her hands on a napkin and reaches into my purse.

"What are you doing?" I ask.

"You have a message. You might have gotten a match," she says.

"A match?" Anson asks.

"Yeah, on the dating app. We uploaded her profile this morning," she answers as she taps on my screen.

I snatch it from her fingers.

"Hey," she whines.

"You know the rules. No phones at dinner," I whisper-yell.

"A dating app, huh?" Anson quips.

"It's stupid. I don't know why I let her talk me into it. I probably won't even get matched," I mumble.

Sebastian grunts, "I bet every guy around here will swipe right on you."

Amiya looks at me and winks. "I know they will," she agrees, then studies him. "What about you? Are you on any apps?" she inquires.

He looks at her and grins a sexy grin. "Nope. I prefer meeting women the old-fashioned way."

"Drunk and desperate?" she asks in mock sincerity.

Anson snorts mid-drink and chokes. Leia reaches over and starts pounding on his back with her tiny fists, leaving greasy prints on his T-shirt.

I put my phone away, and the conversation thankfully shifts from my dating status to the contest at hand.

"I concede," Sebastian finally says as he lays his mallet in the middle of the table and pushes his plate to the side.

"What's concede?" Leia asks.

"It means he's a quitter, LeLe," Amiya bellows.

"He's giving up," Anson confirms.

Her eyes come to me. "So, I win? We get ice cream?"

"It's getting late," I start.

"A bet's a bet. And a man never reneges on payment," Sebastian says.

She looks at him in confusion.

"I'm buying you ice cream."

She smiles wide, her dimples make an appearance, and I swear the three men sitting across from her swoon.

I shake my head.

"Not tonight though. You have a tummy full of crab, and it's getting late. I don't want to be up nursing a tummy ache all night."

Leia's bottom lip comes out, and I glance across to see Sebastian pouting at me as well.

"Stop it, both of you," I demand.

"Tell you what. I'll take you guys fishing this weekend, and we'll get ice cream then. How does that sound?" he asks Leia.

"Can Minnow come too?" she asks.

"Minnow can come too," he agrees.

"Deal!"

chapter seventeen

Sebastian

"AND TO WHAT DO I OWE THIS PLEASURE?" NANA ASKS AS I hop out of my Bronco.

She has a pair of gardening gloves on and a spade in her hand, tilling at the ground around her mailbox.

"Can't a man just want to come by and see his favorite grandmother for no reason?" I ask as I kiss her cheek.

"He can. He usually does not," she notes.

"Gramps asked if I'd swing by and help him open the pool this evening. He'll be finished with his last charter in about half an hour," I explain.

"Oh, wonderful. I was hoping to have it open so Leia and I can swim next week," she says.

At the mention of the little girl, my gaze drifts across the street.

"Avie's having lunch with her director today," she informs me.

I shrug. "I didn't ask," I say.

She gives me a knowing smile. The same one she would give me and my brother and cousins, growing up. The all-wise-grandmother expression.

"Bastian!"

I turn back to the cottage at the sound of Leia's voice and can just make out her mess of brown curls over the fence.

"Hey, squirt," I call as I look down at Nana.

"I'll be right back."

"Take your time," she says as she continues digging in the soil.

I trot across the road and peek into the garden. Leia is wearing a glittery dress with a fairy tutu, a gold-and-pearl crown, and a pair of golden wings.

"What are you doing here, all by yourself?" I ask as I lean over the gate.

"I'm not by myself. Aunt Miya is in the kitchen. See?"

She points over my head and turns to see Amiya watching us through the window. I raise my hand, and she waves in return.

"Wanna have a tea party with me?" Leia asks.

"Tea party? Sure," I say.

She opens the gate and leads me over to the garden table.

"Sit here. I'll be right back," she instructs.

I take a seat, and she skips over to the playhouse and opens the door. She disappears inside, but returns with a tray holding a miniature tea set. She sets it carefully in the middle of the table and runs back. When she comes back, she has a plate of cookies and a bowl of grapes. She sets them beside the tray and climbs up into the seat opposite me.

"Do you want one lump or two?" she asks as she places a teacup on a saucer.

"Two," I request.

She opens the sugar bowl and pretends to plop two cubes in my cup. Then, she holds up a tiny pitcher. "Milk?"

"Please," I say.

Once she has it prepared, she takes the teapot in hand and carefully pours it. I'm surprised when actual tea fills the cup.

"Would you like lemon?"

"I would indeed," I state.

She looks around the table.

"Oh, wait, I forgot. Stay here," she says before hopping down and sprinting back to the playhouse and fetching a bowl of sliced lemons. She places one in my cup and one in her own before pouring herself some tea.

I grasp the delicate porcelain handle, extend my pinkie finger, and bring it to my lips.

"Mmm, refreshing," I praise.

She extends the plate of cookies to me, and I take a Fudge Stripe.

"Thank you, fairy princess," I say.

"You're welcome, jolly giant," she replies.

Jolly giant?

I rest my cup on the table and look at her. "Can't I have wings too? I want to fly."

"You're a boy, silly," she muses.

"Boy fairies don't have wings?" I ask.

She twists her nose. "Wait here."

She jumps down and takes off toward the house. When she comes back, she has her hands full, so I run over to open the gate.

"I don't have brown or green boy wings, but I have these," she says as she enters.

She holds up a pair of iridescent purple wings. I take them from her hands.

"Oh, wow, these are pretty sweet. Think they'll fit me?" I ask.

"Mommy wears them."

"I'm a little bigger than Mommy, but we'll try."

I fish my arms into them and pull them onto my back. The tight elastic straps bite into the flesh under my arms.

I turn my back to Leia and glance at her over my shoulder. Glee is beaming from her face.

"How do they look?" I ask.

She jumps up and down. "Beautiful."

"Just what every fairy man wants to hear," I note.

"They glow in the dark," she advises.

"Really? That's kinda cool. Guess we'll have to hang out until dark so I can test them out."

She settles back at the table.

"So, what's your opinion of Sandcastle Cove so far?" I ask.

Her brows furrow.

"What do you think of the island?" I clarify.

"There's a lot of outside here," she says.

"Outside?"

"Yeah, with grass and trees and sand."

"I guess you didn't see much of that in New York, huh?"

"Only on Tuesday," she replies.

"Why Tuesday?"

"Rita took me to the park on Tuesday."

"And who's Rita?"

"My nanny, silly," she says as if it were the most obvious thing in the world.

"Right, your nanny. I should have known that."

We finish our tea party just as Gramps's truck pulls into his driveway.

"Looks like it's time for me to go, kid," I say as I stand.

"Fly away, fairy prince," she says instead of goodbye.

Then, she takes the tray and flitters off to the old oak tree house.

Amiya appears from the front of the house and meets me at the gate.

"Nice wings," she notes as I exit the garden.

I turn and shake my backside so they flutter in her direction.

She laughs.

I shrug them off, and the relief is instant. I rotate my shoulders a couple of times as the circulation returns to my arms.

Gramps lets out a long, sharp whistle to get my attention, just like he did when I was a boy.

"That's my cue," I say as I hand the gossamer wings to her and head across the street.

"Smart move, by the way," she calls after me.

I turn to face her and begin walking backward. "What's that?" I ask.

"The fastest way to her heart is definitely through Leia," she states.

"Who says I'm after anyone's heart? Maybe I just enjoy a good afternoon tea party."

She folds her arms over her chest and glares at me.

It's an intense staredown that relays everything she wants it to.

I raise my hands in surrender. "Or maybe I'd like to get to know her better."

The corner of her mouth rises.

"Tread carefully, my friend. All knowing her better will do is make you want her *and* her heart even more," she warns before calling for Leia to come in and shower because her mom is on her way home.

I join Gramps in the backyard, and we set to prepping the pool for the season as Nana and Ida Mae sit on the deck, drinking iced tea and supervising.

I spent many summers here in this oasis. The bike ramps and

trampoline have been replaced by a vegetable garden, bursting with tomato and pepper plants, but the pool and firepit hold a ton of good memories. My older brother, Lennon, and I learned how to swim right here with Nana's patient guidance, and my cousin Harry split his head open, jumping off the side into the shallow end during a cutthroat game of Marco Polo.

It was an idyllic childhood. One full of love.

When we weren't spending our afternoons with Nana, we were on a boat with Dad and Gramps. Learning to catch, clean, and cook our own dinner.

Lennon and I both knew how to pilot a boat before we learned how to drive a car. Nothing excited me more than being on the ocean, sailing against the waves and hoping for a big take. Those voyages are where our sense of adventure was born. My brother joined the Navy and spent months at sea, serving his country on aircraft carriers, while I chose a much less noble approach by taking off to California and spending my days playing on a yacht with my friends to quench my thirst.

Once the cover is removed, thoroughly cleaned, and stored in the shed, I check the pump, filter, and heater for any damage while Gramps drags the garden hose over.

We take a break and join Nana and Ida Mae while the pool fills to the proper level.

"Will it be ready by Monday?" Ida Mae asks.

"It should be. I'll measure the pH and chemical balances tonight, and we'll shock it before I leave. Then, tomorrow, I'll swing by and vacuum it well and check the temperature. If needed, we can turn the heater on overnight to get it just right," I say.

"Wonderful. It'll be fun to have a little one splashing around again," Nana says.

"Now, don't you go getting too attached, Nana," I say as I take a swig from my glass.

"Says the man who was sipping tea with a four-year-old a couple of hours ago," Ida Mae retorts.

I cut my eyes to her. "You spying on me, Ida Mae?"

She leans over and cups my face with her cool, frail hand. "Since the day you were born," she says.

It's the truth. Between Nana's watchful observation and her best friend's keen eye, I didn't get away with much, growing up.

Maybe we're all in danger of falling for the girls next door.

chapter eighteen

Avie

"Mommy, hurry!" Leia cries.

I engage the emergency brake on the golf cart, grab the handles of the oversize aqua beach bag and sling it over my right shoulder, grip the sides of the red Igloo cooler I packed full of snacks, and sprint after her and Amiya, who are already making their way, hand in hand, under the arched wharf sign.

We find Sebastian and Anson hosing down the deck of one of the larger fishing boats.

"Bastian, we're ready," Leia squeals, her lemon-print swimsuit covered by a hooded yellow terry-cloth dress.

She's wearing white framed sunglasses that match the bow in her hair. Amiya painted her toenails pink this morning, and she was excited to show them off in her new open-toed sandals.

When she makes it to the dock, she reaches her arms in the air so Sebastian, who has tossed the hose back onto the dock, can scoop her up and set her on the boat's deck.

"Minnow," she cries as she darts for the puppy who's sunning on the deck.

Amiya follows suit and raises her arms.

Anson obliges and hastens to lift her up and over the threshold.

"You need help with that?" Parker asks as he comes up the pier behind me.

"Thanks," I say as he takes the cooler from my hands and steps ahead of me.

He boards and sets the cooler aside before turning and offering me his hand.

While the boys ready us for takeoff, I cover Leia from top to toe with a layer of sunscreen as she squirms while Minnow attempts to lick her free of the thick lotion.

"Need some help?"

I look up to see Sebastian grinning as he watches me struggle to control the two of them.

"You can hand me those," I say as I eye the life jackets.

He passes one to me and commands Minnow to settle while he secures the smaller one on Leia.

Once we're outfitted, I pull her into my lap and come to rest on the leather-covered bench seat under the canvas shade.

Sebastian takes a seat at the helm as Parker and Anson untie the ship and push us off.

Leia squeals as the motor roars to life. I scoot to the edge of the bench, bringing her with me so she can reach the railing. Her hair is tousled by the wind as she leans over and takes in the sparkling water. I tighten my arms around her waist as she enjoys the thrill of her first real boat ride.

Conrad and I took her on the Staten Island Ferry a few times, and she loved it, but that can't compare to being in a motorboat on the ocean.

Amiya plops down beside us as we pick up speed.

Parker takes over the wheel, and Sebastian joins us.

He crouches down to Leia's level, his eyes sparkling with genuine affection as he points out the different sights. "Look there. It's a pair of dolphins."

Her eyes widen with delight.

"Mommy, do you see them?" she yells.

"I do."

Sebastian's patience and warmth are evident as he continues to tolerantly answer her endless stream of questions, his deep voice carrying above the hum of the engine.

"Is the water going to get calmer?" Amiya shouts as she clings to her wide-brimmed sun hat.

"We're taking you guys to a sandbar a few miles offshore to fish. We'll be there soon," he replies.

"So, we're not going out very far, then?" I ask, slightly disappointed.

He raises an eyebrow at me. "You want to go deep sea fishing?"

Before I can answer, Amiya interrupts. "No, sunbathing on a sandbar while you guys fish sounds amazing."

His eyes come to me. *Another time*, he mouths.

I grin up at him.

"Fishing off the bar will be a little more Leia's speed," he explains.

"Yeah, you two will have to do an adult-only fishing trip next time," Amiya says as she waggles her eyebrows at me.

We arrive at the sandbar, the boys secure the boat, and we make our way to a spot by the water.

Parker and Anson set up a tent while Sebastian unloads the fishing gear.

Amiya and I carry the cooler and beach bags to the tent, where we spread a large sand-proof Turkish blanket. I help Leia out of her vest, and she slings her sandals off in the sand. Then, I force her to let me reapply lotion to her neck and face, much to Minnow's dismay.

There's only a couple of hours left before the sun starts to set, so Amiya and I peel off our cover-ups and lather with tanning oil before settling in to watch the boys and Leia.

Sebastian drives four PVC pipes into the beach, about six feet apart, while Parker and Anson come behind him with rods, and Leia and Minnow supervise.

Once everything is in place, Sebastian leads Leia to one of the rods and bends down to show her how to attach a lure. The bright, spiky contraption makes me nervous, but he's careful as he helps her handle it safely.

"You can stop holding your breath. They are professionals," Amiya notes.

She's right. I'm sure they have taught children to fish many times.

I relax back onto the towel I've rolled up to use as a pillow and close my eyes, enjoying the sound of the waves and the way the salty breeze kisses my sun-warmed skin. Trusting them to look after my young one.

I nearly drift off when Amiya calls for my attention.

I look up to see her peeking over the top of her lowered sunglasses and follow her gaze to the water's edge, where Sebastian is reaching for the hem of his T-shirt, his muscles flexing subtly beneath the fabric. With a swift motion, he peels it from his body, revealing bronze skin, glistening with a sheen of perspiration.

"Damn," she murmurs as the shirt slips from his fingers.

Minnow promptly snatches it from the ground and runs toward us.

Her eyes come to me. "You lucky bitch," she says.

I open my mouth to protest when she shakes her head.

"You're crazy if you don't take that man for another spin. Look at him."

I do indeed cast my eyes back in his direction and watch as he ties his hair up out of his face.

A shiver runs down my spine as I imagine the feel of his beard as he kisses his way down my throat. A tantalizing mix of roughness and softness as his stubble grazes my skin and his hands cup my face.

I sigh.

"Exactly," she says with a laugh as Minnow drops the damp tee in between us, does a few circles, and then snuggles in on top of it. "Even the puppy thinks he's delicious," she says as she reaches down and scratches his ear.

I groan. "I really need to stop," I mutter as I throw my head back down to the towel and cover my face with my forearm.

"You know, I caught him in the garden, having a tea party with Leia the other day. It was the most adorable thing I'd ever seen."

"What? When?" I ask.

"When you were lunching with the turtle lady. One minute, she was playing by herself, and the next, I heard her chatting away with someone, so I peered through the window, and there he was, wearing a pair of wings and sipping from a tiny little cup."

"That's …"

"I *know*. All that preciousness from the man who gave you the best night of your life," she muses.

"That's a bit of a stretch," I mumble.

"Okay, but it was definitely in your top two," she states.

"I'll give you that," I agree.

"You know, I think I might take Anson for a spin."

"What?" I gasp as my head snaps to her.

She rolls over onto her stomach and lays her head on her folded arms, facing me. "He's cute, right?"

"I guess so, but what about the guys you've been dating from the app?" I ask.

"Dating is a bit of a stretch. I'm not marrying anyone. I just figure if you can have a hot island hookup, so can I."

"No one is hooking up," I stress.

She grins. "Not yet," she muses.

"Not ever," I insist.

"I give you another week before you cave," she quips.

"Cave to what exactly?"

"His charm. You've piqued his interest, but he's being cautious. As soon as he decides to dial it up a notch, you're a goner," she says.

"Are you saying I have no willpower?"

She smirks. "You have the willpower of steel. You've had exactly two lovers your entire life. Which is mind-blowing. What I'm saying is, that man is sex on a stick, and you're already hot for him. So, why not indulge? Again."

"You're incorrigible," I accuse.

"Guilty as charged. I plan to *encourage* the hell out of you."

I just shake my head as I close my eyes.

Poor Anson has no idea what's coming for him.

chapter nineteen

Sebastian

As I kneel by the water's edge, I watch the sunlight dance on the rippling surface, casting a golden hue over the tranquil ocean. Leia is standing beside me, her wide eyes full of wonder. It's a privilege to teach the art of fishing to such an eager pupil.

"Are you ready?" I ask, smiling warmly as I hand her a small fishing rod.

She nods, her tiny hands clutching the pole with determination. "Yes. Can we catch a big fish?"

I chuckle. "We'll sure try."

With gentle guidance, I show her how to hold the rod and cast her line into the water. Her giggles fill the air as she struggles to mimic my movements, and her enthusiasm is infectious. I remember how exciting it was the day Dad and Gramps took me fishing for the first time.

"Like this," I say, demonstrating the proper technique. "You have to be patient and wait for the fish to bite. Sometimes, it takes a bit for them to come around."

We back up, place her pole in one of the anchors, and take a seat in the sand behind it.

She crosses her arms over her knees and focuses on the line. We sit in silence for a while, the only sound being the gentle lapping of the water against the shore and Parker and Anson's occasional chatter.

Leia's excitement begins to wane as the minutes pass by without any action.

"I don't think the fish like me, Bastian," she says, her bottom lip quivering slightly.

I scoot beside her and place a reassuring hand on her shoulder. "Fishing takes time, kiddo. Sometimes, you have to wait for the perfect moment."

Determined not to let her spirits dampen, I decide to change tactics. I reach into the bait box, pull out a small worm, and dangle it in front of her.

"Would you like to try baiting the hook?" I ask, a playful twinkle in my eye.

Her face wrinkles up as she takes in the wiggly creature before she decides to be brave and reaches for the worm.

I pull it back.

"Not so fast. Watch me first," I instruct as I take one of the spare poles lying on a towel and attach the worm. "Remember, just like with the lure, you have to be careful not to poke yourself."

"I can do it," she boldly states.

I grab another worm from the box and hand it to her.

She giggles as it twists in her closed hand. Then, with careful concentration, she threads it onto the hook, her tiny fingers working diligently.

"There you go, Leia! You're a natural," I praise, admiring her determination. "Are you sure you aren't a fisherman?"

She shakes her head.

"I think you are now," I say as I ruffle her hair. "Remember how to cast?"

With the bait in place, she casts her line once more, her eyes scanning the water with anticipation. Minutes tick by, but this time, there is a newfound sense of patience in her demeanor.

We remain standing, and I help her keep her balance in the wind as she keeps a tight grasp on the rod.

And then it happens.

"Bastian, I think I got a fish!" Leia exclaims as the small pole in her fist begins to jerk.

I watch as her hands tighten around the rod, her face alight with joy as she feels the tug on the line. Carefully, I help her reel in her first catch—a small sunfish, gleaming in the sunlight.

Her eyes widen in awe as she holds up her prize, a radiant smile spreading across her face.

She turns, holding the line with the catch hanging off the end. "Look, Mommy. I did it! I caught a fish!"

Avie's head pops up from the blanket, and she blinks a few times before her eyes adjust. When she sees her daughter bouncing on the balls of her feet, she gets up and comes sprinting to gush over her catch.

"Wow! Would you look at that? A fish on your first day. That's amazing," she praises.

Pride swells within me as I watch her and Leia's exchange, knowing that I played a small part in this unforgettable moment.

Together, the three of us gently remove the fish from the hook and release it back into the water, watching as it darts away beneath the surface.

"I'm so proud of you, squirt," Avie says as she wraps her arms around Leia's shoulders.

As the sun begins to dip below the horizon, casting a warm glow over the sand, we all retire to the tent, and Avie and Amiya empty the contents of the cooler and spread a buffet of meats, cheeses, and crackers across a towel for us all to enjoy while we watch the sunset.

Parker and Anson make their way back to the water to pack up our gear, and Amiya follows to dip her toes into the sea.

Leia curls up in her mother's arms, and her eyelids grow heavy.

"You know, this day will be etched in her memory forever. Just like the first time my dad and Gramps took me fishing," I say.

Avie threads her fingers through Leia's curls.

"Mine too," she whispers and then sighs.

It's a sound of contentment.

Days like today are a reminder of the simple joys that are found in teaching and learning. A joy that is too often lost aboard our charters, where we have to cope with arrogant or drunken idiots. Moments like this are why I love it so much.

By the time we make it back to the marina, Leia has caught her second wind and reminds me that I owe her ice cream.

Parker helps me get the boat settled in while Anson is in the back of the boat, huddled under a blanket with Amiya.

"They look cozy," Parker states.

They do indeed.

"Think I'm going to head to the bar tonight and see if I can find a stranger to wrap herself around me tonight too," he says.

I grin at him.

We both know he's going to sit in the corner and watch Audrey.

"Good luck," I say.

"I guess that means you don't want to join me," he notes.

"I owe a cute girl ice cream. She's earned it today," I say.

He looks over his shoulder to where Avie is unhooking Leia's life jacket.

"Today? She earned it when she wiped the floor with your ass with those crab legs," he scoffs.

"That too."

He hands me the rope, and I tie us off.

"Go on. Get out of here. We'll get the rest," I tell him, and he shouts his goodbyes to everyone.

Avie takes Leia's hand, and they walk up beside me with Amiya and Anson on their heels.

"Since it's getting a little chilly out, why don't I take Amiya and Leia home in the Bronco and you drive the golf cart?" Anson suggests.

"No," Leia starts to protest.

Amiya tugs one of her curls.

"Don't worry, LeLe. They'll stop and get your ice cream while we get you into a bath to wash the sand and sunscreen off. We'll cuddle in our pajamas and have ice cream while we watch a movie."

Leia must like that idea because she lets go of Avie's hand and takes hold of Amiya's.

Avie reaches into the bag resting on her shoulder and hands a key chain to her friend.

chapter twenty

Avie

"HERE WE ARE," SEBASTIAN SAYS AS WE PULL INTO THE PARKING lot of Beaches & Cream.

He parks in front and turns off the ignition.

"Ice cream. Not exactly an exciting Saturday night nightcap for you," I note.

"Are you kidding? I love ice cream, and we can take it home and share it with Leia. I owe her after all," he says.

He hops out of the golf cart, and I follow him to the walk-up window.

"Welcome to Beaches & Cream. It's the best ice cream on the island. Others claim to be homemade, but Beaches is the only one to actually make their ice cream from scratch every day. Simple ingredients. Great taste," he explains.

"Wow, you sound like a commercial," I muse.

"I might have worked here a summer or two when I was in high school," he says.

"Hey, Sebastian. What can we get for you tonight?" the portly gentleman inside the window asks.

Sebastian leans against the wooden bar underneath the opening and turns to me. "What do you think? The Ocean Liner?"

I glance at the handwritten menu on the six-foot-tall chalkboard to our right. Under the heading for Banana Splits is a list of five options, starting with The Raft, which consists of half a banana, one scoop of ice cream, one topping with whipped cream, and a cherry on top; to The Titanic, which consists of three whole bananas, ten scoops of ice cream, ten toppings with whipped cream and cherries.

"The Ocean Liner has five scoops of ice cream. There's only four of us and a tiny human," I point out.

"Right. I forgot about Amiya and Anson," he says as he turns back to the employee and slaps his hand on the bar. "Better make it a Titanic, Roy. To go."

"Sebastian, we'll never eat all of that!" I cry.

He pulls his wallet from his pocket and pays the man before turning back to me. "You've never seen me and Anson destroy a pint before. Besides, if we don't finish it, I'm sure I can think of something to do with the extra whipped cream and cherries," he whispers in my ear.

A thrill runs down my spine at his insinuation.

Instead of shrinking from his obvious flirting, I return his serve.

Batting my lashes in his direction, I bite my bottom lip.

"Sorry, but I have the best friend bunking with me tonight," I break to him before walking around the corner of the building to the pickup window.

"Dammit, I should have gone for the nightcap at my place," he mutters as he follows.

A teenage girl with braces hands us a white paper bag.

"Enjoy," she says cheerfully.

I dig a ten-dollar bill from my wallet and drop it in the tip jar on the ledge as Sebastian loads up on napkins and plastic spoons from the cabinet by the picnic tables.

Sebastian chooses to take the long way back to the cottage, using the back road that follows the coast of the Intracoastal.

I find myself scooting into the heat of his side as I hold the doggie bag of frozen goodness in my lap. He lifts his arm onto the back of the seat and curls his hand around my shoulder, shielding me from the chilly breeze.

The moon is high in the sky and bathing the road in soft light as we cruise past the stilted homes with lit docks.

It truly is beautiful here.

Sebastian's fingertips absentmindedly tangle in my hair as I lean my head against him and close my eyes.

For a moment, I let myself enjoy the feeling of being in his arms, surrounded by the scent and warmth of him, and remember the sight of him above me as he moved inside me.

The look of desire in his eyes and the strength of his hands as they roamed my body.

A shudder runs through me, and his grip tightens, causing me to moan.

He makes an abrupt right turn into Waterside Park. It's closed for the night, and the gravel lot is shrouded in darkness.

"What are we doing?" I ask as I sit up.

He undoes his seat belt and turns toward me. The hand that was holding the steering wheel comes around and cradles my face.

"You can't make sexy little sounds like that and expect me not to notice," he murmurs.

"I didn't," I start to protest, but the words die on my lips as his mouth finds mine.

Our lips connect, and I'm instantly liquid in his arms. He moves the hand on my shoulder to the small of my back to keep me steady, and the movement deepens the kiss. When his touch hits the skin above my shorts, I'm lost. Electricity sparks down my spine, and I instantly drop the bag to the floor of the cart and lift my arms, wrapping them around his neck. I open my mouth and melt into the kiss. He pulls me in even closer until I'm tucked tightly against him.

I'm not sure how long we make out like teenagers, but by the time we finally separate, my lips feel bruised.

On impulse, I crawl across the bench seat and into his lap. The steering wheel bites into my back as I wrap my arms around his neck and dig my fingers into his hair, pulling it loose from the tie.

His hands fall on the outside of my thighs that are resting on either side of his legs.

I tug his mouth back to mine and start to move against him as his tongue gently laps at mine.

I feel his cock growing hard beneath me, and I bear up to reach between us.

That's when another set of headlights pulls into the parking lot.

"Shit," I gasp as I try to move off of him quickly, scraping my back against the metal of the steering wheel.

I cry out at the same time the horn blasts.

Sebastian grabs my hips and halts me.

"Relax," he says as he holds me.

I pull away. "They saw us," I whisper.

"Who cares?" he says.

I rest my head against his chin as the car makes a tight loop and pulls back on the road in the opposite direction.

"See, they were just turning around," he says as he licks the skin just below my ear.

"Sebastian," I moan as his hand slips between us.

I start shaking my head.

"They're waiting for us," I say as I grab his wrist.

He groans, but he brings his hands up to grasp my sides. He plants a quick kiss to the corner of my mouth and lifts me.

My back screams.

Once I'm back in the passenger seat, he turns the key and starts to back out as I reach down and grab the ice cream bag. Thankful it seems to still be intact.

We ride the rest of the way to the cottage in silence.

Once we are parked in the garage, I exit, but before I can reach the door to the house, Sebastian stops me. He lifts my shirt and gently runs a finger over my skin, and I wince.

"You have an angry-looking welt," he says.

I look over my shoulder at him.

"Worth it," I whisper, and his eyes heat as I grab the doorknob and yank it open.

chapter twenty-One

Sebastian

I'M NOT SURE HOW I MANAGE TO PULL MYSELF TOGETHER ENOUGH to sit at the island and share a banana split with her daughter, but I do.

Leia's eyes were as big as saucers when she got a look at the massive dessert that Avie served in a casserole dish with five spoons.

Afterward, the little girl talked me into sticking around while they watched *Moana*.

Which made me think about Hawaii. Yeah, I'm that fucking pathetic that a kids movie can send my hormones into overdrive.

Watching Anson and Amiya covertly paw at each other under a blanket on the love seat doesn't help matters either.

Thank goodness the torture is short-lived when Leia falls asleep twenty minutes into the flick.

Avie carries her to bed, and I leave the other two in the living room while I excuse myself to the kitchen and rifle through the fridge in search of a beer.

No luck.

I grab a soda and make my way back to the recliner just as Avie appears from the hallway.

"All tucked in," she says softly.

She looks around the room.

"Want to watch an adult movie?" she asks.

That causes me to grin, and she blushes. A beautiful rosy pink.

"I don't mean an *adult*, adult film. I mean, a normal adult movie," she sputters.

That makes us all burst into laughter.

"Shhhhh," Avie says as she turns and looks back toward Leia's door.

Anson stands.

"Thanks, but I think Amiya and I are going back to my condo to have a couple of drinks."

He looks down at her for confirmation, and she extends her hand to him. He takes it and pulls her to her feet.

"Okay, so just us, then," she says as she looks nervously at me.

"Um, Seb is our ride," Anson says.

"Right. I forgot you brought the Bronco," I mutter as I start to stand.

"Um, sit," Amiya demands. "We can take my car. That way, I'll have a way back in the morning."

"Are you sure?" Avie asks her.

Amiya gives her a mischievous smile. "Positive. You two enjoy your adult film," she coos as she leads Anson to the front door.

Once the door shuts behind them, her eyes come to me.

"Netflix?"

I bite my lip to keep from making a joke about chilling.

"Sure," I say instead.

She picks a remote up from the coffee table and tosses it at me. "I'm going to go change into my pajamas. You choose a movie."

I move from the chair to the couch and flip through the

recommended options on her account, and I'm pleased to find the first *Aquaman* on the list.

I click play and settle back into the cushions when she appears in a silky blue shorts set. I slide over to make room for her beside me, and she joins me, pulling a blanket from the back of the couch and covering us both.

After a few moments, she relaxes against me.

When the end credits run, I look down at Avie, who is now sprawled out with her head resting on my lap.

"How's your back feel?" I ask as I run my fingers through her hair.

"Fine," she says as she closes her eyes.

"Let me see."

She sighs and rolls over, grabs the hem of her shirt, and raises it so I can inspect her skin. The welt has gone down, but in its place is an angry-looking purple mark.

I trace it with the tip of my finger.

Then, I lean over and press a gentle kiss to the injury.

She purrs at my touch, and the sound causes my body to come to life. She notices immediately and lifts herself off of me.

I catch her by the waist.

"Leia's asleep down the hall," she mutters.

I look up at the hallway. Then, I stand, taking her with me. I set her on her feet and grab her hand.

"Come here," I instruct as I tug her toward her bedroom.

"Wait," she starts to protest but follows me anyway.

Once we're in her room, I lead us into the walk-in closet, closing the door behind us.

"Sebastian," she gasps as we are encased in darkness. The only light coming from the gap at the bottom of the door.

She presses on a light under one of the shelves holding an insane amount of shoes as I push her up against it.

"Say it again," I demand as the soft glow from the light illuminates her.

Her eyes go soft as her back meets the wood. She wraps her arms around my neck and bears up on the tip of her toes.

"Sebastian," she whispers against my lips.

I groan as her teeth rake over my bottom lip.

Taking her arms, I raise them above her head, and she clasps the shelf above her. I pull her forward just slightly to make sure her back isn't hurt.

Then, I slide down her body, kissing the slip of creamy skin exposed by her lifted shirt.

Once I'm on my knees, I tug the hem of her sleep shorts and drag them down her legs as she watches.

Her eyes darken with desire as she steps out of them. Her chest heaves with anticipation as I run my hands slowly up her calves.

A hum of pleasure vibrates from her throat as I slide a finger into her panties.

She sighs in relief as I insert a finger, gliding it through her wetness.

"You're ready for me," I say, and I lift my finger from her and suck it into my mouth.

She lets out a groan as she watches me lick her flavor from

my finger before reaching up and pulling her panties down her legs.

For a minute, I just stop and look at her.

"You're so fucking beautiful, Avie," I say hoarsely.

I spread her legs wider apart and run my nose up her core, inhaling deeply as I hook one of her legs over my shoulder and bring my mouth to her. Using my tongue, I run a line right through her swollen folds, and her hips buck forward.

"God, you taste good," I whisper against her.

Then, my tongue goes up and twirls around her clit, and she cries out before letting go of the shelf with one hand and covering her mouth.

The sound is music to my ears.

I suck her bud into my mouth and insert a finger inside of her.

She starts grinding her hips into my face, wanting more, grabbing my hair and demanding it faster, harder, deeper.

I add another finger as I feast on her.

"Oh my God," she moans.

I devour her until she explodes in my mouth, like a bomb going off. Her legs begin to quake as her grip on my hair tightens, and she holds me to her.

I lap at her, drinking in every drop, and continue to pump my fingers in and out until her muscles loosen and she lets out a satisfied sigh.

She lets go of the wood, and her entire body goes limp. I catch her in my arms as we crumple to the closet floor.

"That was …"

"Delicious," I finish for her.

I brush her hair away from her damp face and kiss her deeply.

My cock is screaming to be released, but I know now isn't the time for more. As much as it pains me, I pull us to our feet. She tags her panties and I lead her out into the room.

She looks anxiously at the bed.

"I'm going to go," I say as she pulls her panties back in place.

"You don't have to," she starts.

I cup her face. "Yes, I do. Because if I stay, I'm going to fuck you until neither of us can stand, and Leia doesn't need to wake up to that sight in the morning," I say before kissing her once more.

Then, I turn on my heel and don't stop until I'm out the door and in my vehicle.

chapter twenty-two

Avie

LEIA WAKES EARLY AND CRAWLS INTO THE BED WITH ME. I DON'T resist and open my arms wide for her to curl up beside me. I know that these days are limited. I'll blink, and she'll be a teenager I'm unable to pry from her bed to get her to school on time.

So, I cherish this time.

When Amiya walks in the door, I'm flipping French toast in a frying pan while Leia watches from her stool at the island.

"Good morning, sunshine," I say as she mumbles something about coffee.

I lift my chin toward the pot on the counter, and she mutters, "Bless you," as she shuffles to the cabinet for a mug.

"Auntie Miya, where did you go?" Leia asks as she fills her cup and takes a gulp.

She plops into the stool beside Leia. "I went for a jog. Exercise is good for you," she says as she pats Leia's head.

"Exercise before breakfast?" Leia questions.

"Yes. I don't recommend it."

I plate the toast and sprinkle it with a dusting of powdered sugar before placing it in front of both of them with a pot of warm maple syrup.

Amiya pours a generous coating on her toast.

"How was your night, kid? Did you like having your bed to yourself?" she asks.

"I slept with Mommy," Leia says around a mouthful.

Amiya's eyes come to mine. "You did, huh?"

"Yep. We watched cartoons in bed this morning till our tummies got hungry. It was fun."

"It sounds like it, although not as fun as my night and morning," she says with a smirk.

I stick my tongue out at her.

She throws her arms out, as if to say, *What happened? I threw you the perfect pitch.*

I shrug and tip my head to Leia.

She just shakes her head and continues to shovel food into her mouth.

Leia finishes and asks if she can go outside and play. I glance out the window and see the storm clouds rolling in, so I tell her to take her coloring book and crayons on the back porch.

Once she's out of earshot, Amiya begins to quiz me. "What happened when we left?"

"We watched a superhero movie," I say.

She grunts.

"And then he ate me out in my closet," I add.

She spits coffee across the island.

"Ew," I cry as I tear a paper towel off the rack under the cabinet by the sink.

"You should have led with that. How was it?"

"Pretty hot. Conrad wasn't really into that," I say.

"Yeah, I know. He sure was into you doing it for him though," she says in disgust and rolls her wrist at me—a prompt to keep going.

"And that was it. He left, and I went to bed. About an hour later, Leia crawled in with me."

"That's it? He just left?"

"Yep. He said he didn't want Leia to find him here in the morning."

"He's a giver," she says. An impressed smile on her lips.

I place my hands over my face. "I feel so bad. He was hard as a rock when he left," I mumble.

"Please, he probably relieved himself before he even made it home," she scoffs. "I'm sure he'll be happy to let you make it up to him."

I look up. "He did text me this morning. He wants to take me to dinner tonight. Just the two of us."

Her hands go into the air. "Thank goodness. Use me before I have to go back to real life."

"So, you don't mind?"

"Nope. And you'd better not sneak back in here until morning," she commands.

Amiya takes a nap to recover from the hangover while Leia and I spend the afternoon at the beach.

I explain that Sebastian and I are going to dinner and she and Amiya are going to make homemade pizzas and finish watching *Moana*.

"Okay," she replies.

"You're okay with that?"

She looks at me funny.

"I like pizza and *Moana*," she says like it's no big deal.

We head back to the cottage so I can shower and get ready for my date.

My date. Oh God, that sounds … scary.

Once I'm showered and I finally decide on a flowy white boho maxi dress and tan sandals, I head to the kitchen and open the fridge to find a Tupperware dish holding chicken salad and grab the loaf of bread from the counter.

"What are you doing?" Amiya asks as she catches me mid-bite.

"I'm pre-feeding," I say once I swallow.

"Pre-feeding?"

"Yeah, he's taking me to that nice restaurant on the beach that everyone raves about, and I want to enjoy my meal," I explain.

"Come again?"

I put the sandwich on my plate and wipe my mouth.

"If I'm too hungry when we get there, I'm going to inhale my food, but if I'm not hungry, I'll take the time to savor it."

"You're a little insane—you know that?" she asks.

I do.

I finish my snack and help her get the ingredients together to make the pizzas before I call Leia in from the garden. I tell her to behave for Amiya and kiss her good night in case she is already asleep when I return.

She promises to listen to her aunt, and as I leave, she is already sitting on top of the island while the two of them begin constructing their pies.

For just a moment, I wish I were building one with them.

Being a single mom and having any life outside of your child is hard. You want and need time with others, but your heart aches when you're away from them.

I meet Sebastian at the restaurant because his last charter for the day is cutting close to our reservation time slot.

When I pull in, he's standing in the parking lot, leaning against his Bronco.

Damn, the man looks good in casual clothes, but he can wear the hell out of a pair of slacks and a button-up linen shirt too.

I check my lip gloss in the mirror before I exit my car and make my way to him. His eyes drink me in as I approach.

"I like that dress," he says as I stop in front of him.

Instead of replying, I walk into his arms and kiss the scruff on his jaw.

He wraps an arm around my shoulders and leads us to the restaurant door.

chapter twenty-three

Avie

WE'RE SEATED AT AN OUTDOOR TABLE FACING THE OCEAN. Twinkling lights hang above us and sway in the breeze.

After we place our order, we fall into easy conversation as we await our meals.

"So, you like it here? In North Carolina, I mean," I ask as our drinks arrive.

"What's not to like? We have mountains and beaches. Four pronounced seasons. Churches on every corner. If they legalized weed, it'd be the most perfect state in America," he says.

"I didn't peg you as a pothead," I say.

"I've dabbled, but I'm a law-abiding citizen now," he says, a glint of amusement in his eyes.

I laugh.

"But seriously, it's home," he says.

"But it's not yachting in the Pacific and spending summers in Hawaii," I note.

"I never intended on doing that forever. The plan was always to run the business with Dad and Gramps someday, and after Dad's diagnosis and Gramps turning seventy, I knew it was time to come home."

"Sebby seems pretty spry to me," I say as I take a sip of my wine.

It's delicious.

"He is. It'll take more than a milestone birthday to take that old bird down. But he prefers the inshore fishing these days."

"Inshore fishing?"

"Yeah, he captains most of the charters that take advantage of the network of fishing spots around the Intracoastal side of the island. He sails his clients into the sounds, creeks, jetties, inlets, and even into the marsh areas to catch flounder, redfish, black drum, sheepshead, and speckled trout. It's great for families. He knows all the best nooks and crannies with the least amount of wind and boat traffic."

"So, he handles the mild waters, and you do the unpredictable ocean?"

He nods.

"He'll bring them around from the backwaters to the beachside if they do a full-day charter. But they stay inland and do some nearshore fishing on the Atlantic side. He even feeds them a nice lunch. He's all about the experience."

I twirl the stem of my glass. "What about you? What's a day on the water with you like?"

He grins. "You should come out with me sometime and find out for yourself."

"I just might do that," I say.

His grin turns to a smile that reaches his eyes. "Atta girl."

I can feel the blush crawl up my neck at his tone.

"What would a day of fishing with you entail?" I ask.

"Well, on a charter, we go about fifteen miles offshore, where the cobia, mahi, king mackerel, and amberjack are. If everyone does well and there's no severe seasickness or anything, I'll take you deeper. Approximately fifty-two miles offshore is ideal for wahoo, mahi-mahi, and schools of bonita. The bonita are fun to catch because when they sprint, you have to wrestle them to get them on board."

I quirk an eyebrow. "Is that the farthest you go out?"

He leans forward. "No, for our more experienced anglers, I'll take them sixty miles out to the reef, where they can catch grouper, in addition to wahoo, and mahi-mahi."

"Hmm, sixty miles—that's quite a jaunt," I muse.

"Oh, but the best is bluewater, and that's around seventy-five miles off the coast. It's only for die-hard fishermen. Out there, you can catch much larger wahoo and mahi or the coveted sailfish. Maybe even a blue marlin. Although they're hard to get."

"Have you gotten one?" I ask.

"Me? Several."

"And how much would a trip to the big-game fish cost me?" I ask.

He steeples his fingers and stares at me. "That's a full-day charter. You'd have me and the boat all to yourself. It's usually about twenty-five hundred dollars."

I whistle low. "Twenty-five hundred. Whew, that's a little rich for my blood," I say.

His eyes burn into mine. "I'm sure we could work something out in trade."

"I don't know. Maybe a nice, long inshore day with Sebby is more my speed."

"I guarantee I'm exactly the right speed for you," he whispers as the server arrives with our entrées.

"What about you? Do you plan to return to New York when you leave Sandcastle Cove?" he asks as the server tops his rib eye with fresh ground pepper.

He thanks them, and they offer pepper to me for my shrimp Alfredo.

"Yeah, maybe. I got the apartment in my divorce, and if my boss at the New York State Department of Environmental Conservation has it his way, I'll be back before Thanksgiving. I'm just not sure," I say.

I do love the charming two-bedroom loft Conrad and I purchased right after Leia was born. It's in a great neighborhood, close to food and transportation. I was grateful he didn't fight me for custody of the prime location. Guilt is the driving factor, I'm sure. Over the next few years, we acquired a couple of other investment properties; they are being sold off, and then the proceeds will be divided between us. I could sure use some of those funds right about now.

I shake the thoughts from my head as I take a bite of the pasta and wash it down with another sip of cabernet. It's divine.

"Is that what you want? To go back to work with them?" he asks.

I shrug. "I'm torn. They do great work, but it's all bureaucratic. That's why I started the PhD program to begin with," I admit.

"You're a doctor. That's impressive."

"No, not yet. I'm working toward it though," I reply.

"What got you interested in marine science?"

"Friends of my parents owned a small house on Tybee Island, and they let us borrow it a couple of weeks every summer when I was little. I loved the ocean. I was obsessed with dolphins, whales, sand dollars, and seahorses. I don't know. It was so different from Atlanta. Even though it was only a four-hour drive, it felt like it was a completely different world. I dreamed of living and working there someday. I guess the career path kinda chose me from there."

"And a doctor was born."

"Again, not a doctor—yet," I clarify.

"Leia takes after you," he states.

"You think so? I think she's her father's spitting image," I say.

"You mean physically?"

"Yeah."

"Physically—I'll take your word for it. But she loves boats and the water and fish, so she's your mini me in every other way. A neat kid. You've done a great job with her."

His praise washes over me like warm honey.

"Thanks. She's my world."

"As she should be."

"As she should be."

The words mean more to me than he realizes.

"You're so lucky you get to do something you love every day," I say, changing the subject.

"I know. I bet you're gonna love working with the turtles too."

"I'm sure I will. But it's just a temporary contract."

"Yep, then it's back to the desk job. Yuck."

"Exactly," I agree.

"So, don't go back," he states matter-of-factly.

"It's not that simple."

"Sure it is. You are the boss of your life. Like the tides. Low to high, high to low. Ever-changing. That's how you should live your life. Ebbing and flowing and never staying static and getting bored."

"Easy for a fisherman to say," I quip.

He shrugs. "Seems like a simple choice for everyone to me."

We fall into a comfortable silence as we both enjoy our plates. All the rave reviews of this place were on point. The food and drinks are amazing, but the real star of the evening is the magnificent view.

When the server shows up with a dessert menu, Sebastian makes two decadent selections and orders them to go.

His gaze meets mine across the table. "Breakfast."

Anticipation bubbles inside of me at the declaration.

The check can't come soon enough.

chapter twenty-four

Avie

HE WALKS ME TO MY CAR.

"My place is down the road. It's in the middle of a renovation, but the views are amazing if you want to check it out," he says as he opens my door.

"I'd love to," I say as I take a seat in the Corvette.

He leans down into the window.

"Just follow me," he says before trotting back to the Bronco.

I pull out of the parking lot behind him, and he leads us to a small beachfront cabana. It's a one-story, built on stilts, with an expansive deck that faces the ocean.

"Sebastian, this is gorgeous," I say after I pull in beside him.

"It's a work in progress, but it's home," he says as he takes my hand in his and ushers us to the steps.

I lean over the railing and watch the tide as he unlocks the door. Moonlight dances across the water, and when I turn around, Sebastian is leaning on the doorframe, watching me.

"Wine?" he asks.

"You have wine?"

"Bought it this afternoon, just for you," he says as he steps aside so I can enter.

The house is indeed a construction zone, just as he described. Everything is covered in plastic and tarps, and the kitchen is a shell.

I walk a circle, taking in all the details.

"I have a lot of work to do. I'm doing it myself, one room at a time," he explains.

"It's got great bones," I say as I run my hands over an old driftwood mantel above the fireplace.

He opens a bottle of wine and turns in search of a glass.

"Sorry, I don't have any wineglasses yet. Or any glasses for that matter."

"This works," I say as I grab the bottle from the counter and take a huge gulp of liquid courage.

He nods and fetches a beer from the fridge.

"Come on. I'll show you the rest of the place," he prompts, and I take the bottle with me as we head down a hallway.

There are two unfurnished, good-sized bedrooms to the right with a Jack and Jill bathroom between them. A laundry room sits at the end, beside a linen closet, and on the left, he opens a door to a large, finished master suite, complete with a massive California king bed, dresser, and chest with two nightstands. A fifty-inch flat-screen television is mounted on the wall opposite the bed. Simple, nice, manly.

I take another sip from the bottle before he takes it from me and sets it on the dresser.

He slams the door shut and then prowls toward me, backing me against it until I feel the cool wood against my skin.

His hand tangles into my hair and twists.

My alcohol-fueled bravery nudges me to take hold of his shirt and twist it in my fist as I pull him to me.

"So eager," he whispers across my lips before his tongue darts out and licks my top lip, then sucks the bottom between his.

The sharp bite of his teeth into my flesh causes a flood of warmth to rush between my legs, and I gasp.

Sebastian takes the opportunity to slide his tongue against mine, and I moan as we begin to wrestle for control of the kiss.

My hands walk their way up his chest to his neck, and then I thread my fingers into his silky hair and tug hard.

He breaks his mouth from mine, and his fiery blue eyes dance with excitement.

"You want it rough, Doc? I'll give you rough."

He grabs hold of my waist and carries me to the mirrored dresser against the wall beside the bed. Then, he turns me so I'm facing my reflection. His hands glide up my rib cage, taking the hem of my dress with them.

"Raise your arms for me, Doc," he commands.

I lift my arms, and he takes the garment and tosses it to the floor. I'm standing before him in nothing but my lacy nude bra and panties.

He snakes his right arm around my abdomen, brings his fingers between my breasts, and nimbly flicks the clasp loose. The silky fabric separates, and my creamy mounds bounce free. Gooseflesh pricks at my nipples to form hard pink peaks as the cool air hits them.

"Fuck," he mutters as his hand takes the weight of my right breast.

I arch back against his chest as he squeezes and kneads the sensitive flesh. I can feel his cock growing hard against his zipper and pressing into my back, and I feed my arm around so I cup him.

His hips move away from my touch.

"Uh-uh. No, you don't," he rasps, and I bring my confused eyes to his in the mirror.

His hand leaves my chest, and he grasps both of my wrists and leans me forward. He places my palms on the wood.

"Grab hold," he demands.

Confused, I clutch the edge of the dresser.

"Don't let go," he says before releasing me, grabbing my hips, and yanking them back slightly.

"What are you doing?" I ask breathlessly.

He takes hold of my hair and sweeps it behind my shoulder, and his mouth comes to my ear.

"Punishing you," he utters before he bites down on my earlobe, causing my head to loll to one side.

"For what?"

"For leaving me that night. I woke up with my cock as hard as granite and reached for you, and you were gone without so much as a word."

I start to defend my actions, but the words fly from my head as his fingers trail, whisper light, between my thighs and find my panties.

He cups my sex, and I can feel the hot liquid escaping as he massages me with the palm of his hand.

Damn, that feels good.

I relax down on his wrist and whimper.

"You're so fucking wet, Doc. Is all this for me?" he asks as his hand slides back, and his fingers skim over the soaked silk and lace.

"Yes," I moan as he circles and then pinches my clit.

He takes a step back and clenches the sides of my panties, yanking them down.

I glance down between my legs at my discarded underwear.

"Avie, look at me," he orders.

My gaze flutters up to his in the mirror before I attempt to look away. Feeling way too exposed.

He grips my chin.

"Look at me," he says again.

I focus on his stare as he gently wedges a knee between my legs to widen my stance.

"I want to see if the blush on your cheeks matches the color of your sweet little pussy," he whispers.

My knees go weak. I have to grip the wood harder to keep myself upright.

He grasps my right leg and feeds it behind his, and I hook his ankle with mine. Then, his fingers find the seam to my opening, and he caresses it, sending a shiver through my body.

With two stealthy fingers, he opens my lips and glides them through my wetness.

"Mmm, pinker," he sighs.

"Sebastian." His name is a cry as I watch his thumb circle me.

I need him inside of me so badly. Every nerve ending in my body is on fire.

He kisses a trail from my shoulder up to my throat as he inserts a finger inside of me and begins to pump it in and out in a maddeningly slow rhythm.

I twist my neck so that I can devour his mouth. This kiss is full of angst and want. Begging him to give me what I need.

He growls. It's a deep, guttural roar from his chest, and his fingers fall from me.

No.

Before I have a chance to voice my dismay, he picks me up off my feet and carries me to the bed. He tosses me on my back and stands between my legs. His breath comes in short, quick pants as his arm goes up, and he grabs the ends of his hair and tugs.

I let my knees fall to the sides, and his jaw tics as he watches me touch myself, trying to relieve the intense pressure building inside me.

His eyes go feral as he drops to his knees. He feeds his hands under my hips and grabs my ass, pulling me to the end of the bed.

"Keep touching yourself," he says roughly.

I do as I was told, and he watches me for a few seconds before his tongue joins my efforts. It circles my clit and then sucks it firmly, causing me to buck off the bed. His grip finds my hips and holds me down while he teases me with his lips and his teeth.

My hand falls away as he takes over. Licking and feasting on me like I'm the best meal he's ever tasted.

I watch as his calloused finger enters me and does a delicious swirl, hitting just the right spot. He slips another in, and I begin to roll my pelvis to meet his thrusts. Riding his face as he devours me like a starved man.

A man starved for me.

The thought, combined with the efforts of his delectable mouth, cause me to crest the wave of pleasure that has been gathering at the base of my spine, and I scream his name as I flood his mouth with my release.

Sweet release.

chapter twenty-five

Sebastian

I CONTINUE TO LAP AT HER UNTIL THE QUAKING IN HER BODY SETTLES.

Fuck, she's beautiful when she comes.

When her breathing evens out, I stand. Her eyes are closed, and she brings her legs up and curls into a ball.

I grin at the sight of her relaxing like a satisfied kitten.

"Uh-uh-uh, Doc. I'm not done with you yet," I say.

Her eyes flutter open as I slide the zipper of my slacks down and spring my rock-hard cock free.

I wrap my fist around it as I reach across the side of the bed to the nightstand to retrieve a foil packet. Placing it between my teeth, I tear it open.

"I'm going to fuck you so good that you won't have the strength to leave this bed before morning," I tell her.

Her gaze never leaves my erection as she plants her feet into the mattress and pushes herself higher on the bed.

Once I'm sheathed, I kick out of my pants and join her on the bed, prowling up her body.

"Promises, promises," she utters as I hook one of her legs behind my back.

"Oh, baby, that's a fucking fact," I assure her as I rake my teeth over one of her taut rosy nipples.

Her back arches, and she moans as I knead the other breast while sucking the stiff peak into my mouth.

They're slightly bigger than I remember. Full and supple. Fitting perfectly into my palms.

Her fingers dig into the tense muscles of my back as I lavish her tender flesh with attention before kissing a path down to her belly button. I bear up and kneel between her knees. She comes up to an elbow and watches as I take my cock in my hand and bring the tip to her entrance.

I tease her. Sliding it up and down her glistening slit. Coating myself with her wetness.

"Sebastian."

"What, baby? Tell me what you want."

"I want you inside me. Right the fuck now," she cries.

At her demand, I move over her, and her arms come to my shoulders. I take her mouth, and she kisses me back. More urgently than before as I thrust into her, slowly at first, until her muscles contract around me. I groan and move my hips, pounding into her.

"I want you to still feel me inside of you tomorrow," I grit out as I pepper her neck with kisses and increase my rhythm.

The smell of her skin, the feel of her breath against my neck, the way she purrs when the scruff on my face scratches her cheek, the salty taste of the sweat beading on her upper lip, and the way her eyes dilate as she gets closer to orgasm all mingle together and drive me fucking wild.

I continue to rock inside of her and shove my hand between us so I can massage her clit. It's exactly what she needs, and her muscles tighten around my cock. It's exquisite torture. She digs her nails into my ass as her orgasm hits, and she cries out my name while I coax every drop of pleasure from her.

I steadily pump in and out until her whimpers give way to

trembling. Then, my back arches, and a guttural growl escapes me as my release follows, and I empty myself before collapsing on top of her, completely spent.

She reaches up and starts to run her fingers through the damp hair at the nape of my neck. "Thank you."

I raise my head and give her a questioning look.

Her mouth quirks into a sexy grin. "For keeping your promise."

Fuck me.

I leave her lying naked in the middle of the bed as I stride to the attached bathroom to dispose of the condom and fetch her a warm washcloth.

When I return, she's on her side, hugging one of my pillows, and she's fast asleep. Setting the washcloth on the nightstand, I slide in behind her and pull the thick navy comforter over us.

The sound of her muffled breathing, combined with the physical exertion, lulls me under too.

The alarm on my phone starts blaring, and I roll over to beat it silent, but when I reach on the nightstand for it, it's not there.

It stops a minute later, so I roll back over, and my body stops against something soft and warm. My arm goes around her, and I pull her back against me. She sighs and nuzzles in closer, the movement causing my body to come to life. My mouth finds her neck, and just as I'm about to taste her skin, the annoying fucking sound blasts out again.

I jolt up, looking around the room for my phone when I realize it's not my alarm.

Avie groans as her eyes flutter open. "Make it stop."

"I would if I knew where it was coming from," I say.

Her hand comes up and points somewhere in the direction of the end of the bed.

"My phone's in the pocket of my dress," she says.

I crawl down until I can reach her discarded clothing. I search for the phone and stop the alarm, noticing that it's four o'clock in the morning.

What the fuck?

"Why is your alarm going off this early?" I ask as I fall back down beside her.

"I wanted to make sure I was back in the house before Leia woke up," she says sleepily as she tucks herself closer to me.

My hand travels over her hip and down between her legs.

She spreads for me, and I clasp her leg and feed it over mine, opening her to me. I tease her with my fingers, getting her ready, as I kiss a trail down her collarbone and across her shoulder until she starts gently rocking.

I reach behind me to retrieve a condom and bear up to roll it on.

"I like having you in my bed in the morning," I growl as I enter her from behind.

She moans loudly as I start fucking her slow and lazily while my hand finds her puckered nipple and starts to roll it between my fingers.

"I like it too," she whimpers before her muscles start to spasm around me, and she milks my cock until I'm spent.

I kiss her neck.

"That was much better than waking up to an empty cabin on a yacht."

She rolls to face me as I collapse on my back.

Her head rests on my chest.

"I thought you needed to get up?"

"Five more minutes," she murmurs.

chapter twenty-six

Avie

I STUMBLE OUT OF THE CAR AND MAKE MY WAY INSIDE. I FUMBLE my way to my bedroom, using only the glow from my phone to light my way. I crawl in beside Amiya and sigh as I snuggle into the soft mattress.

"How was your night?" Amiya whispers into the darkness.

"Memorable," I mutter.

"I can't wait to hear all about it before I leave."

I groan. "Do you have to go?"

"Yes. I don't live here, remember?" she mumbles. "Besides, you start your new job tomorrow. You'll be too busy to miss me."

"I don't want you to go and leave me here alone," I whine.

She wraps her arms around me. "Don't cry, lover. I'll be back before you know it," she teases.

"You'd better be."

We both fall back to sleep for about an hour before we feel a tiny body wiggle its way between us.

"Are you guys having a slumber party?" she asks groggily.

"Yep, and if you want to join us, you have to be very quiet," Amiya mutters as she wraps her arms around her.

"Okay," Leia agrees.

"So, what are we going to do on our last day before Auntie Miya has to go home?" Amiya asks as we eat our bacon and eggs.

"The beach!" Leia shouts.

"The beach, huh? I guess I could use a few more tan lines before I leave."

She picks her phone up from the table and taps out a message.

"What are you doing?" I ask suspiciously.

"Inviting a friend," she says.

"Who?" Leia asks as she crawls to her knees and leans over to Amiya.

"Anson," she replies.

I give her a scathing glare. She knows if she invites Anson, then Parker and Sebastian won't be far behind. And after our wanton night, I'm not sure I'm ready to see him.

My brain needs time to process.

"Yay!" Leia cries.

My little one has grown fond of those men. The thought scares me a bit. I don't want her heart to break when it's time to move on from here.

"Oh, stop with the face," Amiya says as she plucks a strawberry from her plate and tosses it at me.

"I'm not making a face," I quip.

"Yes, you are. That line between your eyes is scowling at me," she insists.

Her phone chimes with a message as I begin clearing the table.

"What did he say?"

"They have a full schedule today, but if we're still out once they're done, they'll join us."

Relief pricks my skin, and I sigh. I toss the dishes in the dishwasher and look over my shoulder at Leia.

"Let's go get our bathing suits on."

She sprints toward her room, and the three of us change, pack a cooler full of water and snacks, grab the sunscreen, and head to the golf cart.

We drive a bit farther down the beach this time so we can set up near one of the fishing piers. It has a nice set of public restrooms, a tiny market, and a tiki bar. There's a gaggle of teenagers making use of the volleyball net to the left.

We forgo our tent and set up our chairs and blankets under the shade of the pier.

Amiya and I pull our towels into the sun as Leia sets up shop with her buckets and shovels a few feet from us.

"So, about last night," Amiya says as she peers at me from behind her sunglasses.

I tell her all about the romantic restaurant, the amazing food and wine.

"He said that?" she gasps when I recount Sebastian ordering dessert and then declaring it was breakfast.

"Yep."

"Confident bugger, wasn't he?" she asks.

"He was oozing with confidence," I agree.

"So hot," she muses.

I describe his house and its state of disarray.

"But the master suite was finished, and it was magnificent," I mutter.

"I bet it was."

Glancing over to Leia, I lower my voice to a whisper as I go into detail, my voice hitching as I detail being bent over the dresser and the way Sebastian's dominant side appeared. Embarrassed by how obedient I was to his demands.

"Wow," she murmurs.

"I know. It felt like I was coming out of my skin; I was so turned on. More so than I was that night in Hawaii, which I didn't think was possible."

"He's a fucking man now," she states. "A big, strong, feral male. Just what you need."

"I don't need anything," I reply.

"But you want him."

"What I want is to enjoy myself without overanalyzing it. To be free of expectation and disappointment for once."

She grins at me. "My baby girl is growing up. I'm so proud of you," she praises. "This is my influence, you know."

She reaches inside the cooler and pulls out a beverage as I ponder her words.

"I know that look," Amiya says as she pops the top to a beer.

"What look? There is no look," I insist.

"You're falling for him," she declares as she pushes herself up to a seated position. Resting her back against the cooler.

"No, I can't. I mean, I could, but I can't," I tell her.

"Who are you trying to convince?" she asks.

"Both of us."

"Uh-huh."

I sit up beside her and tug the amber bottle from her fingertips and take a long pull. Then, I wipe my mouth with the back of my hand.

"It's easy. Being with him. The conversation and flirting. Even the sex was so easy and fun. Everything with Conrad had been hard. He made everything some sort of test. Was I charming enough at his business dinners? Did my dress and hairstyle look appropriate? Did I appreciate all he gave us enough? Sebastian doesn't care about any of those things. He's the opposite of Conrad in every way."

"Exactly. He's the anti-douchebag."

"Really? He lives in swim trunks and sleeps on a sailboat. You think that is anti-douchebag?"

"He's handsome, unpretentious, and talented. I think that is anti-douchebag," she says as she takes the beer back, "even if he is currently taunting a bunch of kids because he's an overgrown child."

I turn and watch as Anson hits the ball to him, and he spikes it in a teen's face. Then, they do a victory dance while high-fiving spectators on the side of the net.

"No, he's not. He's a man. A real man. One who works in the sun and smells of sweat and salt water when he gets home. One whose touch is rough, like the calluses on his hand, one minute and gentle the next," I muse.

"Uh-huh," she says like she caught me.

"Turns out I prefer a workingman's hand to a soft, well-manicured one," I quip.

"Well, damn, now, I want me a boat captain," she mutters.

"Anson's a boat captain," I say.

"He's too laid-back for me. He's just someone to play with," she says.

"You could do with a dose of laid-back."

"Because they're easy, right?"

"Right."

We spend the rest of the afternoon soaking up the golden rays and enjoying Leia's play.

Amiya looks back at the guys, who are laser-focused on their opponents.

They joined us an hour ago and have already challenged the teens in a cutthroat game of volleyball. Leia is playing cheerleader on the sidelines as she watches the action while the two of us make our way back and forth to the tiki bar.

"That man looks at you like he wants to take another bite out of you," she notes.

I glance over my shoulder, and Sebastian winks at me before his attention is pulled back into the game.

"Anson looks at you the same way," I say.

She chuckles. "No, he doesn't. We had a sloppy one-and-done night. You and Sebastian could be so much more."

"I don't know if I can do that," I say.

She turns to me and gives me her serious face. "Why not?"

"Because every day that we get closer is another day we get closer to the end," I whisper.

The bartender arrives with our fruity concoctions.

"Oh, this looks amazing. Thank you, handsome," Amiya coos, and he rewards her with a bright smile.

He places a cherry on top of each of our glasses and winks before rushing off to help other patrons.

Amiya picks up her cocktail, spins on her stool, and brings the straw to her lips.

"What if it doesn't have to?" she asks.

I turn with her to face the intense volleyball game before us. Focusing on the way Sebastian's muscles ripple with every serve and trailing the bead of sweat that travels down his chest and slips under the band of his low-slung swim trunks.

"What?" I ask.

She shrugs. "End. What if it doesn't have to end?" she asks.

"It does," I insist.

"Why?"

My eyes slide to her as tears begin to prick at the corners.

"You know why," I whisper.

"You could always stay in North Carolina. Sell that stuffy apartment in New York and live off that while you work on your doctorate."

"What happened to enjoying the moment and not overanalyzing?"

She shrugs. "I'm just thinking through all of the possibilities."

"That is literally the definition of overanalyzing," I quip. "Besides, I thought you wanted me to move back to Georgia."

"I do, but what I want more than anything is for you to be happy. And this place is a lot closer to Georgia than New York."

"It was one night, Amiya. Let's not make anything more of it."

"You're going to have to face your fear sooner or later," she says, all levity gone from her voice.

I shake my head.

"It's only gonna get worse, the longer you wait."

I lay my head against her shoulder.

"I know," I whisper.

She grins as she brings her straw to her mouth.

"Maybe I'll give Anson another spin tonight," she says, changing the subject.

Lord help him.

chapter twenty-seven

Sebastian

After we wipe the sand with the adolescents and teach them a lesson in humility, we and the girls make our way down the beach to grab dinner.

"Damn, dude, you like her," Parker says as we take a seat inside the Barnacle Café.

The girls lead Leia to the restroom so they can change out of their wet swimsuits.

"Of course I do. What's not to like?" I admit.

"She is hot," Anson chimes in.

"She's not the hot girl you met on a beach in Hawaii anymore. She's a single mother now," Parker says.

"What does that have to do with her being attractive?" I ask.

"Single moms are just different. They aren't girls you mess with just to get your rocks off," he explains.

I set the menu I was looking over down and glare at him.

"Get your rocks off? What are we, horny teenagers?" Anson asks as he chuckles.

"Yeah, sometimes, I think we are," Parker barks as he tosses a bottle cap from his beer at Anson. "And that's fine, but mothers are off-limits. At least, they should be," he continues as he focuses his attention back on me.

I was there when his father split when we were just kids. I remember how hard it was for Parker. How he tried to step up and be the man of the family for his mom and younger siblings. I also remember the string of losers that his mother brought home in the years after the divorce. Parker even came to blows with one of them and ended up spending the night in jail.

"Park, man, I'm not looking for just a hookup," I begin.

"Been there, done that," Anson mumbles under his breath.

I cut my eyes to him, and he raises his hands.

"Just sayin'."

"Then, what are you looking for? Because I've never known you to be interested in more than casual dating before. And they—Avie and Leia—are only here for a short while," Parker points out.

"I enjoy her company. She's beautiful, and she's interesting, and her daughter is cute as hell. But you're right; they're just here for a few months, so there's no point in starting something with her," I state.

Avie appears from the restroom in a pink tank top, her toned legs peeking out of a pair of tiny white shorts. Her long blonde hair is hanging out of a pink ball cap. She has Leia's hand in hers as she leads the little girl up to our table.

Parker looks over his shoulder at them and back to me.

"I hear you saying one thing, but that look on your face is saying something completely different," he states.

"Um ..." I can't find my words.

Parker snaps his fingers in front of my face and brings my attention back to him.

"For fuck's sake, just be careful with her," he advises.

"I will," I promise as I stand and help them into their chairs.

Once Amiya has joined us, we place our orders, and the server brings a small plate of fries for Leia while we wait.

"So, you're leaving us tomorrow, huh?" Anson asks.

"Yes, I have to get back to reality," Amiya replies as she squirts ketchup on Leia's plate of fries.

"That's too bad," he says.

Her eyes snap to him. "Oh, Anson, are you gonna miss me?"

He places his elbows on the table and turns sad eyes to her. "Like crazy," he whines and sticks his lip out.

She cups the side of his face. "Don't worry, handsome; I'll be back the week of the Fourth for two whole weeks. I'm sure you'll have plenty of summer island bunnies to keep you company until then," she coos.

"What's an island bunny?" Leia asks, and Anson laughs as he taps her nose.

"Cute little bunnies with beautiful, full cotton tails," he says, and Avie growls at him.

It's an adorable sound. Like a lioness warning off a hyena.

Leia looks up at her mother. "Can we get an island bunny?"

Amiya leans over to the kid. "No, LeLe. Island bunnies are cheap imitations of a real bunny. They're fun to play with for a while, but they die off quickly."

"They die?" Leia whimpers.

Avie cuts her eyes to her friend as the rest of us try to hold in our amusement.

Stop, she mouths.

I reach over and snatch a fry off Leia's plate.

"Hey," she cries.

I toss the fry into my mouth and reach for another.

Leia slaps at my hand.

"I'm hungry," I state.

"Get your own fries," she tells me.

I sit back and fold my arms over my chest.

"And I shared my ice cream with you the other night," I scoff.

She looks me dead in the eye. "That was the ice cream that you owed me, and I shared it with you," she declares, all thoughts of dead bunnies gone.

Parker and Anson start hooting.

"Oh, she told you!" Parker wails.

Avie smiles and mouths the words, *Thank you.*

I wink at her as I wave down the server and add a large plate of French fries to go with my wings.

Avie and Amiya excuse themselves to go pack up their things under the pier while we pay. Leia stays behind with us so she can finish her coconut milkshake.

As the four of us walk down the steps that lead to the beach, Leia notices a ghost crab scurrying across the sand.

"Look," she calls as she jumps in the air, and Parker and I take her hands and pick her up.

"Whoa, that was close. It almost got you," Parker says.

"Do it again," Leia requests.

Anson clicks the flashlight on his phone and illuminates the path in front of us, and dozens of the tiny crustaceans scatter. We pick her up again, this time thrusting her higher in the air as she squeals.

"Again," she cries.

We continue to swing her above the sand as we make our way back to the pier.

We come across a beached jellyfish, and Leia wants to inspect it.

"Not too close. It can still sting you," I warn as she leans over the sticky glob.

"It's pretty," she says as she examines it closely.

A little boy walks over, holding his father's hand. When they near the jellyfish, he pulls the boy into his arms and carries him to the surf.

"Daddy, I want to look at it," he whines.

Leia watches them as they make it to the water, and the man dips the boy in and out of the crashing waves.

"My daddy doesn't love me anymore," she says out of nowhere.

"What? Why would you say that?" I ask as I crouch down beside her.

She shrugs. "He went away," she says sadly.

"That doesn't mean he doesn't love you."

"Mommy said he doesn't."

I look up at Parker in confusion.

"She told you that?" I ask.

She shakes her head. "I heard her tell Aunt Miya in the car. She thought I was sleeping, but I woke up."

"I bet you misunderstood them," I tell her.

She looks up at me. "What does miss stood mean?"

Parker picks her up from her spot in front of the blob, bends and sets her on his knee.

"Sometimes, when little ones"—he taps the tip of Leia's nose—"hear adults talking, they don't understand what is being said because grown-ups talk differently than little ones do," he explains.

"But they said Daddy didn't want me anymore. If he loved me, he would. 'Cause Mommy loves me and she wants me."

Parker wraps his arms around the little girl and pulls her into a tight hug.

"Oh, Leia, grown-ups and their feelings can be complicated

sometimes, but you know what? No one could meet you and not love you. I promise you that."

I can see the weight of the words heavy on Parker's face. That's not a promise he can make for Leia's father, but he pours all the reassurance he can into that embrace.

He looks over at me above her head.

His gaze conveys exactly what he's thinking. *This is what I meant by single mothers are different.*

I swallow hard and nod at him. *I get it now.*

chapter twenty-eight

Avie

SEBASTIAN ACTED STRANGE AFTER DINNER. I DON'T KNOW IF IT was the island bunny comments Amiya made or what, but when we invited them back to the cottage for one more movie night before she left, Anson accepted, but Sebastian and Parker declined, saying they had plans to meet friends at the bar later.

Now, I'm not one to read anything into situations like this. People have plans, and they aren't always available. He owes me zero explanation. We aren't dating. We're barely acquaintances. We aren't even acquaintances with benefits. We shared one night. Technically two. Sure, he seemed extremely interested in us the past few weeks, but maybe all he wanted was to, as he put it, "punish" me for cutting out on him once. Now, he's done with me.

That's fine. I'm done with him too.

Still, the entire ride back to the house, I imagine just what kind of "friends" they are meeting.

Anson is no help. When Amiya casually asks about their plans, he just shrugs and says something about a bartender who's hot for them both.

"A ménage à trois perhaps?" she jokes.

"Maybe," he replies nonchalantly.

The thought causes bile to rise in my throat.

Shit, Avie. You can't have caught feelings after one night with the man.

I mentally scold myself as I white-knuckle the steering wheel of the golf cart.

"I didn't figure Sebastian to be that adventurous," Amiya notes.

"More like Parker isn't. Sebastian's always been a playboy, but Parker is a romantic," Anson says.

"Sebastian's always been a playboy."

If I wasn't sure before that getting involved with the guy was a bad idea, that statement from a man who's known him his entire life just drove the point home.

I'm glad he didn't come back with us.

I let the anger drive out the jealousy and floor the golf cart as we make our way down the lamp-lit street.

Leia throws her hands in the air and screams, "Wee," as her hair flies around her face.

Once we're home, Amiya makes popcorn while I get Leia bathed. I only allow her to watch one thirty-minute cartoon before I scoot her off to bed.

She stomps her way down the hall in protest.

"But I'm not even tired," she whines as I tuck her in.

"We talked about this. Tomorrow, Mommy starts her job, and we both have to get up early. So, we have to start going to sleep early now too."

"Are you going to bed?" she asks through tears.

"Yep. I sure am."

She sniffles. "Can I sleep with you?"

I shake my head. "Nope. Big girls sleep in their own beds. At least most of the night. Aren't you my big girl?"

She rubs her eyes with her fist and nods.

Amiya's head pops in, and she comes to sit on the edge of the bed. "Night, kiddo. *Sleep tight; don't let the bed bugs bite,*" she sings as she tickles Leia's feet.

I swat at her. "Don't get her all riled up," I say.

She moves up and kisses Leia's forehead. "I just wanted to say goodbye because I'll be gone by the time you wake up in the morning."

Leia starts to cry again.

Great.

"Hey, stop that and give me a hug. I'll be back so soon that you won't even have time to miss me."

Leia sits up and throws her arms around Amiya's neck. "I already miss you," she mumbles against her chest.

Oh, my heart, Amiya mouths to me as she pulls her in tighter.

"Remember, you can video-call me anytime," she tells her.

We both tuck her in, and I blow her one more kiss before we click off the light and back out of the room, pulling the door shut.

"That kid sure knows how to make me melt," Amiya mutters.

"Yep. She's a pro," I agree. "I'm going to head to bed myself. You and Anson enjoy yourselves."

She squeezes me. "I'll come say goodbye before I head out."

"You'd better."

I enter the bathroom and quickly shower, moisturize my face, and pull on my pajamas. It's the same blue set Sebastian peeled off of me the other night.

Ugh.

Suddenly, I don't want anything that reminds me of him to touch my body. I walk hastily to my room and change into an oversize T-shirt.

Better.

I curl up under the covers and slip off into a fitful sleep.

I'm shaken awake by Amiya.

"I'm heading out," she whispers.

I glance over at the window. It's still dark out.

"What time is it?" I ask groggily.

"Five. I want to get ahead of the morning traffic. If I leave now, I can be at the office by noon."

"Okay. Drive safe and text me when you get there," I mumble.

"I will. Have a good first day," she says, and I roll over and drift off for two more hours.

When my alarm sounds, I jump up and hurry to prepare breakfast before waking Leia.

While she eats her oatmeal and cinnamon toast, I get dressed and throw on some light makeup. Then, I get her ready and walk her over to Ida Mae's house.

She meets us at the door, wearing a terry-cloth robe and house shoes, a full coffee cup in her hand.

"Good morning," she greets.

"Hi, Ida Mae," I say as we enter her cozy living room.

Leia goes straight to the fluffy Persian cat that's perched on the couch and begins to run her hand along its back.

I hand Ida Mae the bag that is slung over my arm.

"I packed a few snacks and a change of clothes in case you need them. I'll be home around five thirty this evening, and I'll come get her right away."

"No rush. We're going to have a great time," she says as she smiles kindly at me.

"I truly appreciate you keeping her," I say.

"You've already said that. Now, scoot. Go enjoy the turtles," she says, shooing me out the door.

Leia doesn't even look up from her new furry friend as I blow her a goodbye kiss.

I lower the top of the Corvette and cue up my work playlist. As soon as "Hall of Fame" by The Script starts blaring through the speakers, I slide my sunglasses on and back out of the driveway, ready to conquer whatever this day brings.

First stop is the beach, where I'll help tape off and secure a new nest that was discovered this morning.

chapter twenty-nine

Sebastian

The season is in full swing. Schools are out for summer, and the island is bursting at the seams with vacationers. Which keeps our schedule jam-packed. Sebby has even put us to work seven days a week for the past few weeks to meet the demand.

I've been so exhausted that I fall right into bed the moment I step on the sailboat.

It's a blessing and a curse to be so busy.

Today is the first day off I've had in twenty days. And instead of heading to my cabana to get some work done, I'm on my way to Nana's house.

She needs a plumber, and since Gramps is working today, I'm the next best option.

I park on the street and go around back to let myself inside.

At the top of the steps, I find a cranky Leia slamming crayons into a tin box.

"Hey there, kiddo," I greet, and all I get in return is a grunt.

I stoop down to look her in the eye. "Why the long face?" I ask.

She frowns, and her hands fly to her chubby cheeks and skim down to her neck. "My face isn't long. It's round."

I chuckle. "I mean, why the grumpy face?"

"Nana said I have to take a nap," she grumbles.

"Really? A nap sounds pretty good to me," I say.

"That's 'cause you're old."

"What? I'm not old," I claim.

"Yes, you are. You're big and old," she growls and stomps her foot.

It's adorable.

I throw my hand over my heart. "Ouch."

"Sorry," she mumbles.

"Sorry for what?" I ask.

"That you're old."

I struggle to keep my laughter choked back as she places her elbows on the table in front of her and rests her chin on her balled-up fists.

"Thanks, kid. Now, let's talk about this nap thing. Naps are amazing. Naps are the next best thing to snacks and toys."

"No, they're not. I'm not even sleepy in the daytime. I'm sleepy at dark."

"Well, I bet if you tried lying down and closing your eyes, you'd find that your body is sleepy and can use a little rest even if you don't think it is."

She shakes her head. "I tried that yesterday. All I do is lie there and lie there and lie there. Then, if I finally do fall asleep, naptime is over, and she wakes me up and makes me mad, and I'm grumpy all the rest of the day. For no reason," she states her case.

"Hmm, I see your dilemma. I get mad when people wake me up too."

She lifts her head, and her arms shoot into the air. "So, we shouldn't do the naps so I don't get grumpy. See what I'm saying?"

"I do," I agree.

Her eyes brighten. "Can you talk to Nana for me?"

"I can. Tell you what. Why don't you and I have a seat on that porch swing, and I'll tell you a story while we wait for her?"

She jumps up from her chair. "Okay."

She sprints over to the swing, and I follow. I reach into my memory for an old bedtime story Gramps used to tell us kids at night as I gently push the swing with my foot.

Leia lays her head against my arm, completely enthralled in my take on pirates and hidden treasure. Before I get to the exciting part, I glance down and see that she is fast asleep.

Careful not to wake her, I slide off, take a pillow from one of the deck chairs, and place it under her head before I go in search of my grandmother.

I find her at the kitchen sink.

"Thank you for that," she says, nodding toward the door that leads out to the deck with a clear line of sight to the swing. "She was in the pool all morning and could hardly keep her eyes open at lunch. I forgot how hard children fight sleep. You and Lennon were the worst," she says, a hint of nostalgia in her voice.

She leans her cheek in my direction, and I kiss it.

"Thank you for coming. I've been missing that face of yours," she says.

"Sorry. Been busy," I tell her.

"Is that the only reason you've been avoiding this house?" she asks.

"I haven't been avoiding it. Your husband has been working us like dogs. If you have a complaint, file it with him."

She hums under her breath. Something she does when she doesn't believe you.

"Where's this leak that couldn't wait for Gramps to get home?"

"It's over at the cottage," she says.

"Avie's place?"

She smiles at the way I worded the question.

"Yes, Avie's place. There has been water on the kitchen floor the last two mornings. She's not sure if it's coming from the refrigerator, sink, or dishwasher. I told her we'd have it looked at."

"Sounds like it might be a bigger job than me and my toolbox can handle," I say.

"Oh, fiddle, you've re-plumbed your entire house," she points out.

"I have, but the appliances were removed first, and I could reach the pipes easily. I also stayed on the boat. Removing her appliances one by one will take days, and I doubt she and a four-year-old can live that long with the water cut off."

"I'm sure you can figure it out quickly," she says as if nothing I said registered.

I shake my head.

"I'll go have a look. Do you have a spare key?" I ask.

She wipes her hands dry on the apron tied around her waist and walks over to the drawer of her china cabinet. She places the key she finds there in my hand.

"Thank you for taking a look. I'll have a hot blackberry cobbler ready when you're done."

I'm elbow deep in replacing a pipe behind the refrigerator when I hear the front door open and close.

I was able to trace the water on the floor to a flooded pan under the fridge. After pulling it out, I could see that the pipe that leads to the automatic ice maker on the door had sprung a leak.

When I look up, a confused Avie is staring at me.

"What are you doing?" she asks.

"Fixing your water problem," I say.

"How did you know about that?"

"Nana sent me," I reply.

"So, you're a handyman too."

"For my grandmother, yes, ma'am."

"Well, I'll get out of your way," she says before turning on her heel.

"Avie, wait," I call.

She hesitates for a moment and then returns. "Yes?"

"How's the job going?" I ask.

"Wonderful."

One-worded answers. Interesting.

"Is that all?" she asks.

I set the wrench in my hand aside and look at her. "Is something wrong?"

Her arms cross over her chest, and she lets out a sigh. "Why would anything be wrong?"

And now, we're answering questions with questions.

I step toward her, and she moves back.

"Are you mad at me?"

"Of course not. Why would I be mad?"

I shake my head. "Never mind. I just need to get the fridge back in place, and I'll be out of your hair," I say.

"What do I owe you?"

"Already covered."

"What do you mean, already covered?"

"Nana promised me blackberry cobbler."

"I can pay you," she states.

"I know you can, but you're not."

She growls at me, "Fine. I'm taking a shower. Lock the door when you leave."

chapter thirty

Sebastian

I SHOULD FINISH WHAT I'M DOING, WALK OUT THE DOOR, GET IN MY vehicle, and drive away.

I should, but I'm not going to. Instead, I leave the refrigerator where it's at and follow her.

It's taken all my self-restraint to stay away from her since my conversation with Parker, and I thought this intense pull I had toward her was under control, but I was fucking kidding myself.

Seeing her all pissed and ready to fight broke any willpower I had been holding on to.

When I push into the bathroom, her surprised eyes meet mine in the mirror.

"What are you doing?" she asks as she turns to face me.

I step into the cramped space, and she steps back.

"You mad at me?" I ask.

"No."

I take another step, and her attempt to move is halted when she hits the vanity.

"Why are you mad?"

Her hands come up, and she pushes against my chest.

I grab her wrist.

"Why?"

"I don't know why," she yells.

"I'm sorry I haven't been around. It's crazy this time of year," I tell her.

"Whatever," she bites out as she looks away from me.

I hook a finger under her chin and guide her eyes back to mine.

"I was an inconsiderate asshole, and I'm sorry. Let me make it up to you."

Her lip trembles as she shakes her head. "You don't owe me anything."

My hand slides from her chin and into her hair.

"Yes, I do. Disappearing on you was a dick move. Whether I'm busy or not, you deserve better, and I'm so fucking sorry. Let me make it up to you."

Her head presses into my hand, and her eyes flutter closed.

Taking a chance, I press my lips to the corner of her mouth. When she doesn't pull away, I do the same to the other side.

She whimpers.

My thumb slides over her bottom lip.

"Sebastian."

My name is a plea, and I cover her mouth with mine and swallow it.

Her body relaxes into me.

I kiss her thoroughly, savoring the taste of her. When we come up for air, she brings her hand between us and holds me at bay.

"I've been feeding sea turtles. I smell like capelin and squid," she says.

"Is that what that is?" I ask as I wrinkle my nose.

She turns red and tries to scoot past me, but I lock her in my arms as I run my nose up her throat and inhale deeply.

"Mmm, nothing turns me on like the smell of woman mixed with fish," I say as I nuzzle her neck.

Her elbow comes up and strikes me in the chest, and I laugh as I stumble backward.

"It was a compliment, I swear."

"Yeah, not a good one."

"Still true," I say as I waggle my eyebrows at her.

She grins as she shakes her head.

"I'm just a man, trying to say the right thing to a woman who thinks she stinks," I insist.

"The right thing would have been a lot less suggestive and skeevy," she quips.

"How about this? I'll carry you to that shower, strip you naked, set you under the warm spray, and soap your body up real good. Then, I'll spend the next half hour meticulously cleansing away any trace of squid guts before I ravage you," I explain as I step back to her. "Better?"

She leans into my touch. "Much."

I lift her at the waist, set her on the vanity, and peel off her T-shirt.

"I'm supposed to pick Leia up from your grandmother's," she says as I begin peppering the tops of her breasts with kisses.

"I'll apologize to Nana for your delay," I say as I continue to undress her.

Once she's naked, I step between her legs, and my fingers go straight to the sides of her face and entwine in her hair.

Tilting her head back, I take her mouth again.

I offer her my hand and help her down and to the shower. I turn on the water and wait until it's warm before I move aside so she can enter.

Stripping out of my clothes, I slide in behind her as she faces the spray, and I take the opportunity to appreciate her backside. I run a hand around her waist and up her chest while I trail kisses across her back.

Reaching for the body wash with my free hand, I pump some into my palm.

She lets my hands explore as I lather her body. Caressing and massaging as I do. Making sure I don't miss a single inch of her skin.

Once I have her thoroughly clean, I place her back under the spray to rinse. Her head falls to my shoulder, and she wiggles her ass against my growing erection. I lean over her and plant a hand on the stall just below the showerhead.

I want so badly to lift her against the cool tiles and fuck her until she's screaming my name, but this isn't about me; it's for her.

It's an apology.

It takes all my strength to stand back up and proceed to shampoo her hair, but I do. Willing my body under control.

Once I'm done washing her, I reach and turn the spray off.

She turns to face me, and my eyes don't leave hers as I grab a towel and start at her feet.

Her hand presses into my shoulder as she spreads her stance so I can gently dry her.

She moans as the terry cloth brushes her inner thigh.

"Don't make those sexy sounds, Doc, or you won't make it to pick Leia up," I warn.

She bites her lip to keep from making another peep as I finish my task, ending with the cloth wrapped around her hair.

Once she steps out of the stall and leaves the room, I dry myself and step back into my discarded clothing.

I meet her in the kitchen, and we gather my tools in silence before we walk across the street, hand in hand.

Nana is sitting in a rocker on the porch with Leia on her lap when she spots us—both of us with wet hair, our fingers intertwined—and a knowing smile graces her face.

This whole thing was a setup.

Cunning old woman.

"Sorry I'm late."

Leia's head snaps in our direction at the sound of her mother's voice. "Mommy!"

Avie releases my hand and catches her as she leaps in her arms.

"I swimmed without my floaties today," she announces.

"You did?"

She nods.

"Yep, and I floated on my back for, like, this many"—she raises both hands and spreads all her fingers wide—"minutes."

"Wow, you're turning into a little fish," Avie praises.

"Nana said you have to learn how to swim before you can turn five," she says.

"That has always been the rule," I say.

I walk over to Nana and place the key she gave me on the arm of the rocker.

"All fixed?" she asks.

And she's not just talking about the pipe.

"Yes, ma'am," I murmur as I kiss her cheek.

"Excellent. Now, who wants cobbler?" she asks as she stands, sliding the key into her pocket.

We all yell, "Me," in unison as we follow her inside.

"You know, your grandfather and I were thinking about taking this out to The Point when he gets home," she says as she pulls the cast-iron pot from the oven and sets it on a trivet.

"What's The Point?" Leia asks.

"Well, Sandcastle Cove is an island with the Atlantic Ocean on one side and the Atlantic Intracoastal Waterway on the other. The Point is the tip of the island where the two meet. It's the best spot to paddleboard, swim, fish, and an even better spot to watch the sunset," Nana explains.

Leia turns to Avie and begins to bounce up and down.

"Mommy, Mommy! Can we go to watch the sunset?" she pleads.

"We weren't invited. Sebby and Sabel probably want to go alone."

"Oh, please, you're welcome to join us," Nana says.

"Please?" Leia begs, folding her fingers together as if in prayer.

"I don't know. It's getting late, and someone has to get a bath and go to bed soon because she has to get up early in the morning to go check nests with her mom," Avie informs her.

"I promise I'll go straight to bed after the sun sits down," she says.

"Leia," Avie begins.

"I won't even need a bedtime story, and I'll get up the first time you ask in the morning."

Avie places her hands on her hips and raises an eyebrow. "The first time?"

Leia nods.

"And you won't be Miss Cranky Pants to Ida Mae tomorrow?"

"Pinkie swear."

Avie looks up from her to me.

"I'll swing by and help Ida Mae and Nana, just in case. Pinkie swear," I offer.

"Don't you have to work?"

"Not until two."

Her eyes shift between the three of our pleading faces.

"I'll grab a blanket and pull the golf cart around," she relents.

"Yes!" Leia shouts, and she throws her hand in the air and turns to me.

I give her a high five, and Avie shakes her head.

chapter thirty-One

Avie

"WAIT, HE WASHED YOU, AND THAT'S IT?" AMIYA'S SHRILL fills my car.

"That's it."

"You were naked and soapy in the shower, but he was a perfect gentleman?"

"Yes."

"Well, that story was anticlimactic," she says.

"Him apologizing and me forgiving him was the climax," I exclaim.

"Oh, sweetie, I was hoping for a much more satisfying climax than that. I bet you were too."

"It was sweet," I insist.

"Uh-huh."

"I'm here. Got to go," I say.

"Call me when you guys get home tonight and give me all the details," she demands.

"You know I will."

"Smooches," she says before clicking off the line.

While we were at The Point last night, Sebastian asked Leia if he could take both of us on a date this evening, so I agreed to take the rest of Glenna's early morning shifts this week if she would cover for me so I could leave early today.

Ida Mae has Leia waiting on the porch, and she takes off running as soon as she spots me pulling into the driveway. I meet her halfway, and she is vibrating with anticipation.

"Are you excited to get ready for our date?" I ask.

"Yes!"

I lead us inside, and I let her pick out her outfit. Sebastian didn't say where we were going; he just told us to dress comfortably.

She picks out a pair of black leggings with blue butterflies, a light-blue tunic with a matching headband, and her navy-blue slip-on flats. I decide to match her in a pair of black leggings, a white tank top, and a gauzy duster. I pull my hair over my left shoulder and braid it. Top it with a black wide-brimmed hat and slip into a pair of ballet flats.

Then, I paint her nails and swipe her lips with sheer pink lip gloss.

She is giddy when Sebastian arrives to pick us up with a red rose for each of us.

He takes a left onto the Westside Bridge that leads off the island.

"Where are we going?" I ask.

"Carolina Beach," he says.

I don't ask why he'd take us to a different beach. Instead, I decide to just sit back and enjoy the evening.

Leia fills the forty-five-minute drive with chatter about her day, but when we pull up to the Carolina Beach Boardwalk and she lays eyes on the brightly lit Ferris wheel, her eyes go wide, and all chatter stops.

Sebastian guides us up the wooden path that leads to the park, bustling with people.

There are street food vendors, carnival games, an arcade, and colorful amusement rides, including the Ferris wheel and carousel.

Sebastian is so patient as he waits in every line with Leia while I snap a zillion photos with my phone.

She chooses a pizza food truck for dinner, and we take a seat at a table with our paper plates and Coke slushies.

I take a bite of the pizza and moan.

"Mmm, that's a hella good pie," I say.

His eyes crinkle as he watches me chew and swallow the cheesy goodness.

"New York ruined you," he declares.

"Excuse me?" I say around my second mouthful.

"You sound like a Yankee now," he teases.

"I do not. You take that back!" I shout.

No self-respecting Georgia girl would stand for being called the dirty Y-word.

"Call them like I see them, Doc," he says with a smirk.

Leia picks at her dinner, but she's all about the cotton candy and kettle corn. Usually, I'd deny her sweets if she didn't eat her meal, but this is her date night, so I let it pass.

"Are you ready to win?" Sebastian asks her.

"Yes! I wanna goldfish!" Leia shouts as she skips toward the game that has small glass globes, containing tiny orange fish, lined against the wall.

He glances at me, and I shake my head and give him pleading eyes.

"You don't like goldfish?" he asks under his breath.

"No."

"You're the worst marine biologist ever," he teases.

I punch him in the side.

"Those things die so easily, and then I'll either have a heartbroken child or I'll have to keep hoping I find it floating before she does so I can replace it," I whisper.

"Hmm, you're right. Traumatizing for all involved. I'll see what I can do," he says.

Leia peeks over the counter to the longneck bottles. "You have to throw a ring onto one of them. It's really hard," she says.

Sebastian bends down to her level.

"It is, and I'm not good at that at all. But you know what I am good at?" he asks.

"What?"

He turns and points to the basketball game behind us.

"And look at the prizes," he says.

She looks over her shoulder and follows his finger from the game to the large four-foot-tall stuffed mermaids hanging from the tented roof of the game.

Her eyes go wide.

"What do you say we try to win one of those instead?" he asks.

She nods enthusiastically.

It only takes him seven tries and seventy bucks' worth of tickets to win the twenty-dollar doll, but he says it was all worth it when he hears the squeal of delight Leia makes as the fella hands it to her.

She insists on carrying the mermaid herself.

And I laugh as I watch her waddling in front of us, trying to keep ahold of the child-sized toy as we make our way back to Sebastian's Bronco.

We don't even make it back on the highway before the sticky, exhausted child is fast asleep, clinging to the prize her Bastian won for her.

I reach over and lace my fingers with his.

"Thank you for tonight. She'll remember it forever," I say.

He slides his eyes to mine and raises our joined hands, placing a kiss on my wrist. "You're welcome."

When we arrive at the cottage, I reach and tug the mermaid from her arms and exit.

I unlock the door while Sebastian picks Leia up and carries her inside.

Leading him down the hallway, I quickly turn her bed down, and he gently lays her on her pillow.

She doesn't stir.

"Wow, she's out," he whispers as I tuck her in and place the mermaid on the pillow beside her.

"A sugar crash," I say as I kiss her forehead.

He follows me back to the living room.

"Nightcap?" I ask.

He shakes his head. "I'd better go. If I stay, neither of us is going to get any sleep," he says as he pulls me into his arms.

I melt into the warmth of his chest and moan as he takes my mouth in a heated kiss.

"Fuck, you make it hard to walk out the door," he says into my ear before nipping at my earlobe.

I shudder.

He places one last kiss on my pulse point before releasing me and backing out of the door.

"Sweet dreams," he says. Then, he's gone, closing the door behind him.

Oh, I'm sure they will be.

chapter thirty-two

Avie

I watch as Amiya drags two large suitcases and a duffel bag up the steps and through the front door.

"Are you moving in?" I ask.

"I'm going to be here for two weeks," she says as she plunks down on the sofa.

"I know, but you're on an island. You need a couple of sundresses and a couple of bathing suits, max," I say.

"Whatever. You know I need options."

Leia bounces out of her room, dragging her new best friend behind her.

"Hey, kid. Where are my hugs?" Amiya calls.

Leia hoists the mermaid onto the couch beside Amiya and then turns so her auntie can squeeze her.

She releases her and looks at me. "What's on the agenda for the day?"

"I figured you'd be tired from the drive and need a nap, so Leia and I are going to go hang out with Sabel at the pool for a while and let you rest."

"God, you're the best," she moans.

"Ariel is going to keep you company," Leia says.

Amiya looks over at the stuffed toy. "Ah, thanks, babe. We can cuddle."

She wraps her arms around the doll and stretches out on the sofa.

"We'll be back in a bit. If you wake up and want to join us, just come over," I say, and she just lifts two fingers in response.

I'm lying on my stomach on a lounger, my eyes closed, listening to Sabel and Leia playing in the pool when a hand slides up my back.

"Hey, sexy. Wanna go for a boat ride and grab lunch with me?" a deep voice murmurs in my ear.

I open one eye and focus on him.

Damn.

"Now?" I ask.

"Yes."

I bear up and look over at Leia. She's wearing her arm floats while clinging to a purple pool noodle.

"I already cleared it with Nana. She's got Leia," he says.

"Okay," I agree, and he takes my hand and helps me to my feet.

I pull a sheer green dress over my bathing suit and let him lead me across the street and down the embankment behind the garden, and I halt in my tracks.

"What is that?" I ask.

"It's a canoe."

"I thought we were going on a boat ride?"

"Hence the canoe," he quips as he tries to tug me forward.

"That's not a boat. It's a floating log, and I'm not getting into it."

He chuckles.

"The waves will topple us," I argue.

"That's why we're staying in the Intracoastal Waterway," he says.

"With alligators?" I screech.

He quirks an eyebrow. "How is it a marine biologist doesn't know that alligators are freshwater animals?"

"Primarily freshwater. They are known to adapt to brackish waters, and I've seen them sunbathing on the banks back here. And even though I find them beautiful, I know enough to not disturb or entice them."

"Scaredy-cat," he teases.

"That's not fear; that's just common sense," I insist.

He extends his hand to me. "Promise you're in good hands. I'll protect you."

"You'd fight an alligator for me?"

"Absolutely," he assures me.

"Where are the life jackets?"

His chin gestures into the hull of the canoe, where two brightly colored jackets are sitting.

"Come on, beautiful," he beckons.

I sigh. "Fine. But there'd better be food on the other side of this adventure."

I take his hand, and as I slide by him, he mumbles, "Worst marine biologist ever," and I give him the stink-eye as he helps me down onto the wooden seat in the front of the craft.

"I don't want to lead," I say.

"You're not. It's just better for the heaviest and the most skilled paddler to sit in the back. Besides, I like the view from back here," he says as he hands me one of the jackets.

I slide my arms in, and Sebastian reaches around me from behind to adjust and secure the straps.

I look over my shoulder, and we are nose to nose.

"I can do that myself, you know."

"I'm just being a responsible captain," he whispers against my mouth as his hand slides from the buckle of my jacket around the sides of my rib cage.

A thrill slithers across my skin.

"There you go," he says before kissing the tip of my nose.

Once we're both strapped in, he hands me one of the single-blade oars and hops out. He pushes the canoe into the water before jumping back in himself and taking his seat at the stern.

We glide through the calm waters of the Intracoastal. The warm, salty breeze kissing our skin as he patiently instructs me in rowing the front of the canoe.

We make our way around the cove to a remote bank, and Sebastian steers us onto the shore, where a blanket is spread in the shade of a tree.

"Did you make us a picnic?" I ask in disbelief.

"Yes—well, the Sandcastle Cove Deli did," he says as he helps me out of the canoe.

"What is this place?" I ask as I take in the tranquility.

"One of my favorite spots on the island. It backs up to the nature preserve. I like to come out here and fish alone sometimes because it's so private and peaceful."

The old oak tree branches dip toward the earth, enveloping us in our own cocoon as we enjoy our lunch in its cool shade.

We lie back on the blanket, entwining our legs as I lie on his chest, plucking grapes from a cluster and feeding them to him.

It's comfortable and cozy.

His finger lifts my chin, and he takes my mouth in a long, lazy kiss.

My hands flutter down his chest and caress the bulge in his jeans.

"I need to get you back to Leia," he says as he breaks our kiss.

"Uh-huh," I agree as I palm his growing erection.

His eyes focus on my hand as he scoots up on the trunk of the tree.

I lean back so he can tug the cover-up over my hips, and he dips and kisses a trail from the bottom of my bikini top to my belly button.

I arch my back as he feeds a hand inside my bottoms.

His eyes stay on mine as he glides a finger through my folds.

"Sebastian," I moan his name as he slides a finger inside of me.

"I love how ready you are for me," he growls.

I writhe against his hand, but it's not enough.

Freeing him from his zipper, I climb on top of his lap and balance my hand on the oak tree above his head.

He takes control, finding my entrance and guiding his cock inside.

"Yes," he groans as I start to move my hips up and down, taking him deep.

Sebastian reaches around my neck, unties the bikini top, and peels it from my breasts as I ride him. He wraps his mouth around a nipple and sucks it between his teeth.

"Oh God," I gasp as he bites down.

I start moving faster as his thumb finds my clit and starts circling it.

"Yes! Oh, you feel so good inside me," I pant as he sucks and tugs.

All the sensations are too much and not enough.

He begins thrusting up to meet my hips, and I clutch his shoulders, digging my nails in and holding on.

That's when he loses control.

He grabs my hips and starts pounding violently into me as my cries grow louder and more desperate. My sex throbs as he pumps harder and harder.

"I'm gonna come, Avie," he grits out, and just the words cause me to tighten around him, and his name explodes from my lips.

He takes my mouth with his and absorbs my cries before he pushes me back, pulls out, and spills his release against my stomach and thighs, and then I collapse on his chest.

Totally worth chancing the alligators.

chapter thirty-three

Sebastian

THE WEEK OF THE FOURTH IS ALWAYS OUR BUSIEST WEEK OF the year. While everyone else is enjoying backyard barbeques, parades, and family time, our team goes hard.

Avie and Amiya bring Leia to the wharf for the Independence Day festivities, but I only catch a glimpse of them as I return to the dock to load and unload charters.

Sometimes, being in business for yourself is a bitch.

This is one of those times.

Avie's long locks are in a ponytail, and she's wearing a distressed tank top with an American flag across the chest and tiny, faded jean shorts that barely cover the tips of those gorgeous legs. I watch as her teeth sink into a candy apple, and then she chases after Leia, who's sporting a star-spangled jumper, and Amiya as they wave lit sparklers in the air.

I want nothing more than to join them.

When did this happen?

When did I become the man who'd prefer to spend the day scarfing down hot dogs and helping a little girl catch the candy being tossed from the parade floats instead of being on the open water, reeling in fish, before going to the bar to hammer beers all night?

I shake the question from my mind as a party of four older men board the dock, ready to wrestle the ocean for a prize catch.

Luckily, the last trip of the evening consisted of a couple of middle-aged dads who wanted to come in before sunset to watch the fireworks with their wives and kids.

This means, if I hurry, I'll be able to catch the island's huge pyrotechnics show myself.

Once the boat is clean and docked for the night, I weave my way through the crowd at the wharf toward our office. It's located in a strip of retail spaces, just past the Boathouse Restaurant.

I tap the code to gain entry and make my way to the set of metal spiral stairs behind the desk to the left of the back entrance. They lead to the rooftop, where I'm surprised to find Avie, Amiya, and Leia with my parents, grandparents, and Ida Mae.

We've spent every Fourth of July I can remember up here, where there is an unfettered view of the Sandcastle Cove fireworks display. Nana pulls out the charcoal grill so one of us boys can fire it up. While she sets up a buffet of potato salad, baked beans, and cherry pie for us to enjoy before the spectacle begins.

This year, my father is the one flipping burgers. The rest of them are lounging in the portable camping chairs surrounding the outdoor rug, where Leia is tinkering with a patriotic-themed pinwheel while Minnow tries to tug it away from her.

I fish a beer out of the cooler and quietly take a seat on it as I watch Avie in deep conversation with my mom. They share a moment of amusement, and something about the sound of their intermingled laughter causes my chest to tighten.

"Sebastian, you made it just in time," Nana calls when she notices me.

"Bastian," Leia shouts as she stands and hurries over to the table that's lodged between Avie and Amiya. She picks an object up and skips to me, Minnow on her heels. "I got you something," she says as she hands me a bright-red-cellophane-wrapped candy-coated apple.

I take the stick from her fingers and hold it up. "You bought this for me?"

She nods. "With quarters from my piggy's bank," she declares proudly.

"Wow, thank you. Candy apples are my favorite," I say as I coil a finger around one of her curls and tug.

She beams at me, and then she and the pup return to her spot on the roof and continue playing with the assortment of trinkets she collected today.

Avie stands and walks over to the buffet table, which is just a folding card table, covered in a red-white-and-blue plastic tablecloth, and refills her wineglass from the bottle perched in a bucket of ice. Instead of going back to her seat, she comes and bumps my shoulder, prompting me to scoot and make room for her on the cooler.

"You look tired," she muses.

I rake my free hand over my face.

"It's been a long day in the sun," I say.

"I bet. It looks like running that charter boat is a helluva workout."

I cut my eyes to her and grin. "You watching me, Doc?"

"Maybe," she whispers.

Dad calls out for a tray, and Mom carries one to him. She unwraps slices of American cheese to top the patties, and then Dad transfers them from the grill to the platter.

"Your parents are nice. Especially your dad. He's funny. He's had Leia laughing all afternoon," she says.

"Yep, he's got a dad-joke arsenal," I quip.

"You two look alike."

"Wait until you meet my brother. He's the spitting image of Dad," I say.

What the fuck am I saying? She'll be long gone before Lennon gets leave again.

She opens her mouth to respond, but before she can say anything, Mom turns, looking around the space.

"Can I get you something, Milly?" she offers.

"Yes, do you see where Mom put the silicone trivets? I don't want to set this hot platter on the plastic."

Avie hops to her feet and walks over to Nana's bag by the table.

I check my watch and notice it's almost eight. The show will start at sundown.

I sure hope Leia and I are able to make it, I think to myself as I watch the girl yawn as she climbs into Amiya's lap.

Mom and Nana begin loading paper plates with all the side dishes while Ida Mae stuffs the buns with meat. I take one from Mom, and Ida Mae drops two burgers beside the potato salad. I finish it off by adding mustard, ketchup, pickles, and onions to each. Then, I walk over to the ledge and use it as a bar while I examine the activity below.

Spectators are sitting on the network of piers, elbow to elbow.

"You want another beverage, Sebastian?" Mom asks over my shoulder.

"I can get it. You don't have to wait on me," I reply.

"I know I don't have to. Now, would you like a cold beer?"

"Yes, please."

Avie is now sitting crisscross on the rug, cutting a patty into bite-sized pieces for Leia to dip in ketchup.

I guess a mom is always a mom, no matter how little or grown her baby is.

The door slams open, and Anson and Parker come barreling onto the roof.

"The party is finally here," Anson bellows.

"You're just in time," Nana says as she hands them each a tinfoil-covered plate.

As darkness settles over us, I make my way to the rug. I lean my back against Avie's, who has returned to the chair beside Mom, her legs stretched out beside Leia, who is doing her best to keep her eyes open as Minnow licks ketchup from her face.

Everyone cheers at the screech of the first rocket jetting above us. It explodes into a dazzling display of light, color, and sound. Sparks, stars, and a kaleidoscope of patterns fill the sky over and over, following the boom, and fizzle down to the water.

Leia curls into my side as she oohs and aahs. Avie's hand finds my hair. Running her fingers through the wind-tangled strands, she gently massages my scalp. It's a small but intimate and comforting act.

I sit here, surrounded by these girls and my family, completely content.

chapter thirty-four

Avie

"What does one wear to a clambake?" Amiya asks from the living room, where she is digging through her suitcases, which have exploded in the corner between the sofa and the front windows.

I peek out of my room and down the hall. "I have no clue. I've never been to one either. It's on the beach, so go with your gut," I call.

Sebastian invited us to join him and the boys for a clambake tonight. They raked in a generous amount of them this afternoon. He even arranged for Leia to spend the evening at the splash pad, followed by a sleepover with his mom and grandmother so we could enjoy a late-night bonfire on the beach.

Rifling through my closet, I settle on a gauzy white minidress and a pair of natural raffia sandals.

I grab a brown leather crossbody and toss in my phone and lip gloss.

"Damn, your tits look amazing in that," Amiya says as I join her in the living room.

The dress is loose and casual but has a dangerously low-cut neckline.

"As do yours," I say as I take in her halter top and low-slung, ankle-length boho skirt.

"We are two hot bitches," she sings.

Two minutes later, a horn blows, and we climb into Sebastian's vehicle with the boys and drive out to The Point.

"Ah, do you smell that?" Anson asks as we exit the Bronco.

"What?" Amiya asks.

"The salty breeze carries the promise of an awesome evening, filled with good food and laughter."

"You're weird," Amiya calls after him.

He grins over his shoulder at us.

With a sense of excitement, we set about gathering everything we need from the back of the SUV.

Then, we head across the sand to the designated spot on the beach where the clambake will be held. It's a secluded area, perfect for our little party, with plenty of space for everyone to spread out and enjoy themselves.

Amiya and I lay out a large tarp to serve as our makeshift dining table, using pins in the corners to ensure that it's sturdy and anchored against the shifting bank, as Sebastian and Anson get to work on digging a hole in the sand. Parker collects a pile of flat beach rocks, and they line the pit with them before tossing in a pile of wood and starting a fire.

Once the blaze is large and the flames are dancing in the pit, the boys peel off their shirts.

"What are you guys doing?" Amiya asks.

"Going swimming," Sebastian quips.

"Swimming? What about the food?"

He grins. "It's going to be a while. The fire has to burn out. Then, we scoop out the ashes, cover the hot rocks with seaweed, add the food, and then cover it with more seaweed and sand."

"What? We cover it with dirt?" she cries.

Sebastian laughs. "Yeah, and it'll cook. Then, we dig it up and dig in."

She turns to me with her hands on her hips. "Did you know we had to bury our dinner?"

I shake my head. "Nope, this is my first time too."

Anson runs up behind her and snatches her cover-up from around her waist.

"Hey," she screams before taking off after him.

Sebastian looks at me and grins as he starts stalking toward me.

I throw my hand up as I start walking backward.

"Oh, no, you don't," I scream.

He takes off in a sprint, and I turn to run, but before I can get very far, his arms come around me, and he hoists me up and over his shoulder. Then, he slaps my behind and takes off for the water as I kick.

We stroll into the surf behind the others.

The warm water laps at my skin as I slide down Sebastian's body just as a wave crashes over us.

The rush of water tosses me into him, and he catches me and pulls me to his chest as I sputter and cough up seawater.

Once I'm stable, I splash him in the face as he reaches out to clasp my waist. I struggle to kick past him, but he has a firm grip on me.

"My dress is all wet, and I lost my sandals," I gripe.

"I'm sorry." He laughs out as he buries his face in my neck.

"You don't sound sorry," I say as I push against him.

He locks his biceps, and I finally give up and wrap my arms around his broad shoulders.

My fingers find the hair at the nape of his neck as I look over my shoulder to see where Amiya is. She's off in the distance, being tossed into the waves by Anson.

I bring my eyes back to Sebastian, and a hidden dimple peeks out of his right cheek.

"Now that you have me, what are you gonna do with me?" I ask.

A glint of mischief fills his eyes.

He takes a huge step, moving us deeper into the ocean, and I instinctively wrap my legs around his waist as we reach a depth that is over my head.

The soaked lace of my panties brushes against his growing cock, causing him to groan deep in his throat.

I close my eyes and tilt my head back into the water as the sensation slivers up my spine.

My tongue darts out nervously, and my breath quickens as I look back at the others once again.

Sebastian buries his nose just below my ear and inhales deeply. I relax my body into him and bring my chin to his shoulder.

He holds me close as the water laps around us.

Then, he places a kiss on my collarbone, and I lean back to give him better access to my throat, which causes the tops of my breasts that are exposed above the deep V of my dress to peek out of the water. He cups one with his hand and gently kneads it.

I close my eyes and moan, bowing my back and bringing the pebbled tip closer to his face. He sucks the nipple between his teeth through the clinging fabric and gives it a rough tug.

I buck in his arms, and he releases it and licks a long, slow trail in the dip of my cleavage. Then, he wraps his lips around the puckered peak once more.

My hips start to rock into his, and as soon as I find the contact I'm searching for, I quicken my movements.

My heat glides up and down his rock-hard erection.

He slides his mouth to the other breast and gives it attention as I continue to glide against his eager cock.

I'm lost in the moment and the feeling of him against me when he bites down on my nipple, and I gasp and raise my head. He skates his hands around my back to my ass and hoists me up, bringing me even closer.

"Give me your mouth," he commands.

I wrap my arms tighter around his neck and do as he asked.

Damn, he's a good kisser.

He takes all of my weight as I lose myself to pleasure again. My body begins to tremble, and his hand finds my clit through my panties. He circles it with his thumb, using the lace to create even more friction as I move against his hand.

My legs tighten around him, and I start to shudder as I get closer. He releases my mouth and leans back so he can watch as I shatter. My cries float into the air and are muffled by the sound of the crashing waves.

"Hey, you two, what's going on over there?"

Amiya's voice drags me from my bubble of ecstasy.

"Avie's just giving me the business for getting her dress all wet," Sebastian yells over my shoulder.

"Assholes. The whole lot of you," she calls back.

Sebastian laughs. A deep, sexy sound as he turns me and leads me toward the three of them.

We play in the surf until the moon is high above us and the flames of the fire have finally gone out on the shore.

Once we are back on the sand and Sebastian offers me a dry T-shirt that goes to my knees, we finish preparing the food.

Sebastian and Parker gather the necessary ingredients for our feast from the cooler. Fresh clams are the star of the show, and the boys pulled the best ones out of the ocean this morning.

I also picked up some corn on the cob, potatoes, and onions to accompany the clams, along with a variety of herbs and spices to season them to perfection.

With everything laid out before us, we set to work, preparing the meal. Sebastian and I scrub the clams clean, removing any grit or sand from their shells, and sort them into batches based on size. Amiya chops the potatoes and onions into bite-sized pieces, ready to be cooked alongside the clams, while Anson and Parker get to shucking and trimming the corn on the cob.

As Sebastian layers the stones with seaweed, Amiya and I arrange the ingredients in large, heavy-duty aluminum foil packets. Each packet contains a generous portion of clams, nestled among the vegetables and seasoned with a sprinkle of salt, pepper, and fresh herbs. Once sealed tightly, they're ready to be placed on the hot coals to cook.

With the food arranged neatly on the makeshift grill, the boys cover it with another layer of seaweed and then dry sand.

I settle back to enjoy the company of my new friends as we wait for our dinner.

The sound of laughter fills the air as we share stories and jokes, passing the time until the tantalizing aroma of cooking clams begins to escape the beach oven and wafts through the air.

Finally, after what feels like an eternity of anticipation, the moment of truth arrives.

Sebastian carefully retrieves the food from the hole, taking care not to burn himself on the scalding foil.

With eager hands, I unwrap each packet, and a wave of delicious aroma wafts through the air, causing my mouth to water in anticipation.

The clams are perfectly cooked, their shells gaping open to reveal the tender, succulent meat within. The potatoes and onions have soaked up the butter and flavors of the sea while the corn on the cob is sweet and juicy.

Sebastian tosses more wood into the now-empty pit and starts a new fire to keep us warm.

With our paper plates piled high with steaming food, we gather on the tarp and dig in with gusto, savoring each mouthful.

"Damn, this is so good," Amiya groans.

"So good," I agree.

Sebastian grins. "Glad to see you're enjoying your first clambake."

"You might have messed up, mister. She'll be expecting you to cook for her all the time now," Amiya says.

As the last scraps of food disappear from our plates and the fire dwindles to embers, I can't help but feel a sense of satisfaction wash over me. The clambake has been a resounding success, coupled with my body experiencing a much-needed release.

With a contented sigh, I lean back against Sebastian's chest and watch as the stars begin to twinkle overhead, grateful for moments like these that remind me that I'm still very much alive and that joy is possible.

For now.

chapter thirty-five

Avie

Ida Mae wasn't feeling well this morning, and rather than disturb Sabel, I decide today is going to be a take-your-daughter-to-work day.

Our first order of business is walking the west side of the beach for nests.

Getting up before dawn isn't fun, but searching for nests is. The reason we go out at daybreak is so we can find the mother turtle's tracks in the sand before visitors disturb them.

They like to lie at night during high tide, and each track is easily identified. They're about forty inches wide, and there are two sets. One made when she is walking from the ocean toward the dunes and one when she returns to the water. The nest, a small mound of disrupted sand, can be found about halfway between.

I opt for the golf cart this morning, and we take the main road to the farthest access point. I unload a heavy-duty all-terrain wagon and toss in my supplies before the two of us walk onto the beach.

Leia brings along her pink sand pail so she can collect shells as we scan the shore.

"You see that fishing pier off in the distance?" I ask.

Her eyes follow my extended finger, and she nods.

"That's how far we have to go. Think you can make it there and back?"

"I can do it."

We remove our sandals and toss them in the wagon, and I pull it behind us as we make our trek.

It's not a small jaunt. The distance from the tip of the island to the first pier is just over six miles. I'll allow her to walk as long as she can, but I made sure to make room in the wagon for her to sit at some point.

She's a trooper, happily keeping up with me, stopping only to gather her sea treasures.

Approximately four miles into our excursion, I spot a set of tracks. I grab my tablet to record the location and drop a pin on the map in my phone as a backup. Then, I measure the nest and carefully stake and tape it off before covering it with a screen.

"There're eggs in there?" Leia asks as she crouches by the nest.

"There sure are. The mommy turtle used her back flippers to dig a deep hole, and then she settles into it and lays her eggs before covering them up," I explain.

"How many are in there?"

"Probably about a hundred."

Her eyes go wide. "She made a hundred babies?" she asks.

"She sure did. And now, we have to watch over them and keep them safe until they boil."

"We're going to boil them?" she shrieks.

"No, when the nest is boiling, that means the eggs are about to hatch, and the babies will dig their way to the top."

She nods her head as if it all makes perfect sense.

By the time we make it to the pier, the coffee shop has opened, so I park the wagon at the bottom, grab the tablet, and lead her up the steps.

The Rest Ashore Café is a small coffee and tea shop that sits on the pier beside the Feelin' Tip-Sea Bait and Beverage Center, and it's one of my favorite places on the island.

The aroma of the freshly roasted beans makes my mouth water as I pull the door open.

A young man stands behind the wooden counter.

"What can I get you?" he asks.

"I'll have a tall iced macchiato with coconut milk and two blueberry scones, please," I order.

He taps on the screen in front of him and looks over the counter and down at Leia. "And what about you, ma'am?"

"I'll have a tall iced chocolate milk, please," she replies.

"You want that with coconut milk?" he asks.

She wrinkles her nose. "Do coconuts come in chocolate?" she asks.

He scratches his temple. "That's a good question. I think they come in all flavors if you want them to," he says.

Leia looks at me skeptically.

"You can make chocolate milk with coconut milk and chocolate syrup or with regular milk and chocolate syrup," I explain.

She takes a moment to consider the options.

"I'll take a regular chocolate milk and make it a really tall one," she decides.

"Good choice," he tells her.

We wait for our order at the high-top table tucked in the corner, and I call Kimball to let her know about our find. She and Leslie are on the east side of the island, working their way to the second pier near the old lighthouse and have identified two more nests.

That's a total of seven so far this season.

I load Leia in the wagon and decide to use the sidewalk by the street to tug her back to the golf cart.

It's a lovely August day, and as much fun as we've had this summer, I'm excited for the coming of fall. The tourist numbers have already subsided as the state prepares for the beginning of the school year.

My heart aches as I note this is the last autumn we have before my girl is off to kindergarten, and I want to soak it up.

Sabel sends me a text when we are en route to the cottage to retrieve my car, telling me to bring Leia to her, so I walk her over before heading to the rehab center for the day.

Kimball calls me into her office right before closing. Which is never a good thing. I check the pH of the holding tank and tell each rescue good night before walking down the hall, tapping on her door and entering.

She's seated behind her desk with the phone to her ear, but she beckons me inside.

I take a seat in the chair facing her and wait for her call to end.

"Is something wrong?" I ask when she rounds the desk and shuts the door.

"No. Everything is fine. I just have some news, and I haven't told the rest of the office yet," she says as she takes a seat on the edge of the desk. "I'm moving on. The National Oceanic and Atmospheric Association Fisheries has offered me a position with Green Turtle Research and Conservation in Southern California starting the first of the year."

"Wow, that's amazing. Congratulations, Kimball," I say.

"Thanks. I'm excited. I'll be closer to my son and daughter-in-law.

He's stationed at Edwards Air Force Base, and I put in for the position when they found out they were expecting."

"Oh, what perfect timing," I gush.

"Yeah, for me and you both."

"Me?"

"The North Carolina Wildlife Resources Commission is looking for a new director to fill my position here at Sandcastle Cove. They asked if I had any recommendations, and I threw your name in the hat."

"You did?"

I can't believe she'd go to bat for me when I've only been working under her for a little over three months.

"But what about the others? Leslie? Glenna?" I ask.

Both have been with the program for over a decade.

"They're great, and both are wonderful at their jobs, but neither of them meets the education requirements for director, and the three of you already work so well together. If you want the job, it's yours."

"I don't know what to say," I mutter.

She smiles. "It's a big decision, and I sprang it on you. Take some time to think about it and talk it over with your family and the New York office. If you decide you're interested, we can revisit the conversation and talk compensation and benefits in a few weeks."

"Thank you, Kimball," I say as I stand.

"I know we're small potatoes compared to the New York State Department of Environmental Conservation, but we do important work here, and it matters. Not just for North Carolina, but also for conservation efforts along the entire East Coast. I hope you'll seriously consider it."

"I will," I promise.

chapter thirty-six

Sebastian

I RECEIVE A PANICKED PHONE CALL FROM AVIE. SHE AND AMIYA HAVE been in an accident off West Beach Drive.

Anson and I leave the sander we're using on the floor in the living room and grab my keys.

Gramps gave us Labor Day weekend off so we could get my floor sanded and stained in preparation for the cabinets and countertops being installed in the kitchen early next week.

He and Parker are handling captain duties with Dad pitching in as crew.

I thought Amiya coming back to town for the holiday weekend would make staying away from Avie and being on task easier.

Sucker.

As we approach the Thirty-Second Street access, we see a frantic Avie waving us toward the right, where Amiya stands beside a white golf cart lying on its side in a ditch.

"How the hell did they do that?" Anson asks as I turn on my flashers and pull up to the scene of the crime.

Avie runs over to my window. "It wasn't my fault. Amiya was flashing some drunk guys standing on the deck of their beach house, and I was trying to get her to sit down before anyone saw us, and while I was distracted, we hit some standing water, hydroplaned, and lost control. I didn't know who else to call. I didn't want your grandparents to see it," she explains without taking a breath.

"Flashing," Anson repeats.

"I wasn't flashing them. I was mooning them," Amiya corrects.

He barks out a laugh.

I shake my head and exit the Bronco to get a closer look.

"Bandits. You two are nothing but trouble," I whisper to her as I pass.

She follows, nervously chewing her lip as I walk around the cart.

"Welp, it's totaled," I say as I throw my hands in the air.

"Totaled?" Avie gasps.

"He's lying. If I had a little more upper-body strength, I'd roll it back over myself," Amiya bellows.

Avie's eyes narrow at me.

I laugh.

"You flipped my grandparents' golf cart."

"Ugh, I know," she whines.

I wave Anson out to help me get the machine out of the ditch.

The damn thing weighs more than you'd imagine, and it takes the two of us a few tries to get it back up on four tires.

Avie hurries around the side to check for damage. The worst of which is a dent over the passenger-side wheel well.

"Park can pull that out," I assure her.

I feel her breath at my ear as she throws her arms around me. "Thank you for coming."

"You're welcome. And don't worry; I won't tattletale. But it'll cost you."

She peeks up at me. Her eyes are dancing with amusement, and the corner of her mouth is curled into a sexy grin. "How ever will I pay you?"

I back her up against the golf cart. "I'm sure I can think of something."

"Get a room!" Amiya shouts.

Instead of heading back to the cottage, Anson talks the girls into coming back to my house for a beer.

Just the distraction we need right now.

Not that I'm complaining.

The two of them do actually pitch in, rolling up their sleeves and mopping the areas we've already rough- and screen-sanded to prepare for the stain.

"This place is cool as shit, Sebastian," Amiya says as she cleans the hallway. "It's definitely a panty-dropper."

Anson chuckles. "Yep, he'll be pulling in all kinds of tail once it's finished."

I lift my goggle-covered eyes to Avie, and she turns away quickly.

I pick up a bottle cap from the floor and chuck it at Anson. He presses his lips together in an apologetic smile.

Avie's leaving, and whatever this is between us is on borrowed time.

I know it, and she knows it.

That doesn't mean he has to be a dick and say inconsiderate shit in front of her while she is here.

Just before ten, Avie looks at her phone.

"We need to get going. I told Sabel we'd be back by ten," she says.

I stand. "I'll get my keys."

"No, you're working. We'll take ourselves back," Avie insists.

"You're not driving the golf cart back to the cove until I've had a chance to check it out and make sure it's okay."

"God, I'm so sorry. You're trying to work, and here you are, having to drive us all over the island."

I lead them out onto the deck and down the steps to the driveway.

"That's okay. You're going to find a way to pay me back, remember?"

She quirks an eyebrow at me. "I thought cleaning for you tonight was me paying you back."

"Come on, Doc. I know you can do better than that," I murmur as I open the passenger door and she slides in.

"You two should go rub one out in the outdoor shower before we leave, or I swear the tension is going to blow the windows out of this thing," Amiya says from the back seat.

Avie turns and sticks her tongue out at her.

"What am I going to tell Sabel about the golf cart?" Avie asks as we walk across the street to retrieve Leia.

"Nothing. I'll have it patched up and back in the garage before she knows it's missing."

"I can't do that. I have to tell her."

"I'll tell her I did it," I offer.

"Why would you do that?"

"Because I'm her grandson, who she loves more than life itself. She is incapable of being angry with me. Besides, do you really want to tell her you flipped it while Amiya had her pants down, wiggling her ass at a bunch of strangers?"

"I guess I'll owe you double."

I grab her elbow and stop her before we round the house into Nana's backyard.

I back her against the house. Bringing my hand up to clutch

her jaw, I rub my thumb over her bottom lip. "I like you being indebted to me, Doc."

She moans as I slide the tip of my thumb into her mouth. She sucks it, and my balls tighten.

"I'd love for this mouth to be sucking something else right now," I whisper as her tongue wraps around it.

Fuck me.

She cocks her head back, and my hand falls. She grins.

"At least, now, I know how to pay one of my debts next time we're alone," she whispers.

I crash my mouth to hers and kiss her breathless as she clings to me. When I break away, her lips are wet and swollen, just like I imagine she is elsewhere.

"We have to go in, or I'm going to fuck you right here, up against my nana's house," I tell her.

"Sebastian," she whimpers.

I take a step back. "Go on. I'll be right behind you. I need a minute."

She does as I commanded and slips past me and into the gate.

Once I've regained my composure, I follow suit and find her coming down the steps with a sleeping Leia in her arms.

"Want me to get her?" I ask.

She shakes her head. "I've got her. Thank you again for the rescue tonight."

I hold the gate open so she can carry Leia home, and then I join Nana, who is seated on the deck.

"I didn't realize you and Avie were out together tonight," she says as I plop down on the rocker beside her.

"We weren't. She called me because she and Amiya hydroplaned in the golf cart and rolled it over into a ditch on West Beach."

She gasps. "Was anyone hurt?"

I shake my head. "Nah, they were fine, and the cart only suffered a dent or two. The only damage was to Avie's pride. She was scared to tell you and Gramps about it, so I told her I'd take the blame."

"How chivalrous," she praises.

"I have my moments."

"She's been good for you," Nana says.

I slide my eyes to her. "I have enjoyed having her around," I admit.

"It's a shame they'll be leaving in a couple of months."

"Yeah, but they have no reason to stay around here, Nana. Sandcastle Cove was just a dot on the map for her. A layover. A transfer. A place to hide and lick her wounds from her divorce. She has a life to get back to."

She reaches up and pats my cheek. "Then, maybe it's time you go give her a reason and a life to stay for."

I shake my head. "I don't know if I have one good enough to keep her here."

"Oh, baby boy, you are more than good enough."

chapter thirty-seven

Avie

"YOU'RE IN OVER YOUR HEAD," AMIYA SAYS AS I EMERGE FROM Leia's room.

"I know."

"It's only going to get harder, the longer you let it go on," she says.

I back up against the closed door. "I'm going to talk to him on Sunday after the picnic and lay all the cards out on the table," I tell her.

"Good. I'd love to be here so I can soothe your broken heart."

I slide my eyes to her as tears fill my vision. "You're always having to bandage me up."

She shrugs. "That's what best friends do. Forever and ever. Now, let's go get drunk and discuss this job offer like responsible adults. We'll do pros and cons. I'll go first. Con: it's not in fucking Atlanta."

I laugh and follow her to the kitchen.

We stay up all night, discussing my next move. Who I should tell, who I should let influence my decision, and exactly what salary point I'd need to hit to make it worth it.

There's no way the rehab center can match my pay at the New York State Department of Environmental Conservation. They don't have the funding and resources, but with the cost-of-living difference, I should be able to afford the cut.

The truth is, if I sell the apartment in New York, I could easily afford to purchase a home for me and Leia in Sandcastle Cove. The housing market here isn't exactly cheap, but in comparison to New York real estate, we'd do well in the move, and we might even be able to purchase a vehicle.

If we unload the other communal property that Conrad and I own, then those funds could go into the bank and provide me with a nest egg and safety net for the future.

I make a mental note to contact my attorney next week to see where we stand with those properties.

The biggest question is, what do I do if the Georgia Aquarium calls? Atlanta is my hometown. My parents and Amiya are there, and that would be a blessing for me and Leia.

I don't want to be that person who accepts a job and then turns around and resigns a month later to take another.

And then there's the Sebastian factor.

I don't even want to let my mind go to what he'll have to say about it all.

Ugh, why does everything have to be so complicated?

Because you deserve it.

I shake the unwanted thoughts and try to get some sleep before Leia wakes up.

I wake up to discover I've slept in, and I find Amiya and Leia in the backyard, where Amiya is attempting to teach her how to hula hoop.

"Mommy," Leia calls when she sees me headed down the steps.

She lets the hoop around her waist drop to the grass and runs to me.

I catch her in my arms.

"We let you sleep for a long, long time," she says as I pick her up.

"You sure did. It's two o'clock already."

"Auntie Miya said you needed the rest."

"I did. Thank you. Did you two have a good day?" I ask.

"Yeah, we made cookies for breakfast," she informs me.

"Cookies?"

"Hey, snitch, that was supposed to be our secret," Amiya huffs.

"Sorry," Leia whispers.

"It's too late to whisper now," Amiya says as she tickles her side.

"We saved you some, Mommy."

"You'd better have."

She wiggles out of my arms and sprints up the steps. "Come on. I'll show you."

"Where did the hula hoops come from?" I ask as we follow her.

"Sabel bought them for her."

"She spoils her."

"Yep, just like a grandmother."

I make a pot of coffee to stave off the raging headache.

And then I get dressed, and the three of us ride out to the park for the local artisan market.

"If I had a beach house, I'd be buying all the things," Amiya muses as we peruse the rows of vendor tents, and Leia sprints ahead of us, chasing a butterfly.

"Don't go too far," I call to her.

I run my hand over an outdoor table made from an old surfboard. It has four attached stools and a foot bar. "I love this. Wouldn't it look good on the pier behind the cottage?"

"Very cool," she agrees.

"Maybe I should get it as a thank-you gift for Sebby and Sabel."

Amiya looks at the attached price tag. "Whew," she whistles.

"That bad, huh?"

"Definitely not cheap."

She turns it around so I can see the number.

Whew *is right.*

"That's another thing to consider. If I do move here, I'll need furniture for a house," I say.

"True. You wouldn't want to haul all that crap from the city down here. It'd cost a fortune. Besides, you don't need to fill a new home with that pretentious crap Conrad made you buy and suffuse it with bad juju."

"Yeah, better to sell it with the apartment. Let the new owners deal with the juju."

"You're seriously considering it, aren't you?"

"I think I am."

She throws an arm around my shoulders.

"Good, because I'm not sure fate could have made its point any clearer."

"Divine intervention," I mutter.

"Divine intervention."

chapter thirty-eight

Avie

"Hey, ladies." Sebastian throws an arm around me and plants a lingering kiss on my lips.

Leia giggles as she wedges herself between us.

Sebastian releases my mouth and looks down at her.

"You're kissing Mommy." She snickers.

He reaches down and picks her up and plants a sloppy kiss on her cheek.

She squirms.

What has gotten into him?

He sets her back on her feet.

"I've got to get back to the dock. You guys enjoy the festival," he says.

I grab his elbow before he runs off. "We're still on for tonight?" I ask.

"Yeah, just the two of us, right?"

I nod. "I want to talk to you about something."

He nods as he backs away. "I need to talk to you about something too. I'll find you when I get back. Should be an early one."

"Okay."

He grins and winks at me before turning and disappearing into the crowd.

"You look like you're about to puke," Amiya says as she joins us and hands Leia an ice cream cone.

"I just might," I agree.

"There's nothing that you can do but let things play out the way they will, so you might as well enjoy the festival."

"That's easy for you to say," I snap.

"It sure is. That's the beauty of only having casual, surface relationships. No nerves. No making myself sick. Just easy-peasy."

"Stop bragging," I grumble.

"Come on, boo. Let's go buy you a cocktail," she says.

"Okay, but I'm warning you: loading the kid up on sugar and me up on alcohol is the recipe for a rough night for you."

A band called The Salty Dogs takes the stage during the picnic, and we spend the afternoon on a blanket, enjoying the music.

Leia makes friends with a girl her age, whose family is lounging beside us, and the two of them dance and twirl while I discuss day cares and the local public schools with her mother.

When Sebastian and Anson find us, the sun has set, and the wharf is lit with strands of bulbs wrapped around every tree and post.

Sebastian slips in behind me and kisses the back of my neck as I sway to the lyrics of the haunting song coming through the amps.

"Having fun?"

I nod. "How was your day?" I ask as I lie back in his arms.

"Good. The last angler caught a sailfish. He was ecstatic."

Leia hobbles over to us.

"Mommy, I have to pee-pee," she whines.

I start to push up, and Sebastian halts me.

"I'll take her. I want to grab a beer anyway."

"If you see Amiya, will you pry her away from the bartender? She went to get us a cocktail forty-five minutes ago," I ask.

He kisses the tip of my nose. "You got it, Doc."

Grabbing Leia, who is now doing the potty dance, he hoists

her into his arms and rushes them into the crowd toward the office buildings.

I lie back and close my eyes. Taking long, deep breaths, I mentally prepare myself for the evening ahead.

A hand caresses my shoulder, and I reach up to lace my fingers with his and freeze.

It's not the rough, strong hand I was expecting.

My eyes fly open.

"Conrad? What the hell are you doing here?" I hiss as I jolt up from the blanket.

"I need to talk to you," he says.

"So, you just show up here?"

"How else do you expect me to reach you? You changed your phone number. I called your mother, and she wouldn't give it to me. Amiya kept hanging up on me. I had to get in touch with your office and sweet-talk one of the interns into telling me you're here, in the middle of nowhere, North Carolina, working on some sea turtle project."

"But why are you here?" I repeat the question.

"I need your signature on some paperwork to sell our property in Long Island," he explains.

"Why didn't you just contact my attorney?"

"I tried. He's on a cruise ship somewhere in the Caribbean for the holiday, and I had to leave a voice mail for his paralegal. The buyer is leaving to go back to Germany in three days," he continues.

"Just give me a copy, and I'll read it over and send it to you," I say as my eyes scan the crowd.

"I've got to head back to Wilmington tonight. I'm on the red-eye back to New York. It took me all damn day to find you."

"You expect me to just sign something you place in front of me without giving me time to read over it?"

"It's a good deal, Avie. He's agreed to the asking price. All-cash offer. We'll split the proceeds fifty-fifty. There's no fine print," he assures me.

Out of the corner of my eye, I see Sebastian heading our way with Leia on his shoulders, her fists clinging to his hair as she giggles.

Shit.

"Fine. I'll sign whatever you have. Let's go to your car," I say as I grab his forearm.

The next ten minutes play out in front of me in slow motion.

"Daddy!"

Leia's voice rings out above the hum of the crowd, and Conrad turns to her.

Anger registers on Sebastian's face as he takes the two of us in.

Anson and Amiya are following behind them, and Amiya's expression is glacial when she spots Conrad.

Dropping the plastic cups in her hands, she races out ahead of the others.

"What the fuck are you doing here?" she screams as she comes to stand between me and my ex.

Sebastian drops Leia from his shoulders and sets her on the ground. She sprints to us, and he follows, keeping a protective hand on her.

I close my eyes as my heart begins to race.

When Leia makes it to where we're gathered, her arms go around Conrad's legs.

Conrad rests a hand on her back, and pain flashes across his face before his attention snaps back to the man who is now standing in front of him.

I watch in horror, unable to move as Conrad extends his hand. "Conrad Sullivan. And you are?"

Sebastian's eyes flicker to his hand, but he doesn't accept it. "Sebastian Harraway."

"Sebastian," Conrad repeats as he turns back to me. "This is him, isn't it?"

"Conrad, please," I whisper.

Amiya bends and pries Leia off of him. "Come on, LeLe. Mommy and Daddy need a minute."

She hoists her up into her arms as Leia struggles against her and hurries toward the boat, where Sebby and Sabel are hanging out, watching the band.

Anson stands at Sebastian's back.

"Sebastian was the name of the guy, right?" Conrad presses.

I don't answer.

He glances back at the two men and focuses on Sebastian's hard stare.

He shakes his head. "She looks just fucking like you."

My ears start ringing as I watch the confusion wash over Sebastian.

"What is he talking about, Avie?"

Conrad's head snaps back to me. "He doesn't know?"

I swipe at the hot tears that are now running down my cheeks.

"He doesn't know," he repeats. "Well, let me be the first to say it, then. Congratulations, Sebastian." He leans into Sebastian's face and sneers, "It's a girl."

chapter thirty-nine

Sebastian

I LEAVE THEM STANDING THERE AND TURN TO WALK AWAY.

"Wait," Avie calls as she grabs the hem of my shirt.

"Avie, what about the contract?" the prick yells.

"I don't care about the fucking contract, you asshole," she roars.

Eyes from every corner of the wharf fly to us. Parents scramble to cover the ears of their children.

In frustration, I turn and pick Avie up at the waist as her ex-husband lunges for her.

Anson throws himself in between the man and us as I turn and walk us toward the charter's office.

I glance at the boat dock and see Amiya seated beside my grandparents, a sobbing Leia clinging to her. Nana's confused eyes follow us until we make it to the door. I set Avie down and punch in the code. Then, I sling the door open and thrust her inside.

"Is it true?" I ask as I prowl toward her.

"Sebastian," she whimpers as she tries to cup my face.

I grab her wrist and push her away.

"Is it fucking true?" I repeat.

"Yes. She's yours," she whispers through tears.

My hands fist into my hair as I try not to lay my hands on her. "What?"

She takes a deep breath.

"Leia is yours," she repeats.

"Mine."

"Yes. I found out I was pregnant six weeks after I joined Conrad in New York. He and I were college sweethearts. We shared an apartment off campus and Hawaii was supposed to be a romantic getaway for the two of us before he started working and I started my senior year, but he was offered an internship in New York right before we were scheduled to leave. He decided to skip out on our vacation and accept the job, then he proceeded to tell me that we needed a break. I was heartbroken. That's how I ended up bringing Amiya along with me to the island. I wasn't expecting to meet anyone there. I just wanted to lay on a beach and lick my wounds. But then I met you and I liked you, so I threw caution to wind. The day after our incredible night together, Conrad began calling and texting me from the city saying he missed me and that he had made a mistake. He asked me to join him in New York as soon as I returned."

"And you did," I surmise.

"Yes. I loved him. I wanted to be with him."

"So, you two married right away?"

"When I told him I was expecting, he proposed. We got married the next month on a Tuesday at two forty-five in the afternoon at the city clerk's office in Manhattan."

Not exactly the wedding every girl dreams of.

"I'm guessing you told him about Hawaii," I snap.

"I did. I mean, not the details, obviously, but I told him I'd been with someone while I was there."

"Been with someone. And he was okay with that?"

She shrugs. "Turns out, he had been with someone, too, so he really couldn't hold it against me. We both assumed the baby was his. I mean, you and I only shared one night together. One reckless night. Conrad and I had been together for three years. What were the odds the baby was yours and not his? We convinced ourselves it just wasn't possible."

"Oh, it was possible. I was there, remember?" I yell.

"I meant, probable. It wasn't probable that it was yours, and we decided there was no reason to find out. We were getting married, and we were raising the baby together. She was our little girl."

"Except she wasn't," I shout.

She winces. "We didn't know that, and everything was amazing at first. He loved her, and she loved him so much."

"But?"

"But … I don't know. We got busy, and he and I started fighting a lot. I finished school while I was pregnant, and when Leia came, I wanted to go to work, and he didn't want me having a job. So, I started working toward my doctorate, and even that irritated him. He wanted a stay-at-home wife to keep his life and home running smoothly. One who lunched and had play dates with the wives of his buddies at the office and who looked pretty when on his arm at company events. I tried. I really did, but I felt like a prisoner in that skyscraper. Then, he suddenly began staying out late, wining and dining clients. Out of nowhere, he grew so distant, and I started getting suspicious. One day, he was in the shower, and his phone started pinging, and something told me to pick it up. They were messages from his secretary. They weren't work-related."

I snort. "He was fucking his secretary? How very unoriginal."

"Yeah, I confronted him, and at first, he tried to deny it. Turned it around and made me seem paranoid and crazy."

"He wanted to have his cake and eat it too."

"I suppose."

"Did you leave?" I ask.

"Nope. Not at first. He pleaded with me to stay, and he agreed to go to counseling."

"The oldest trick in the book," I spit.

"It got better for a while—it really did—but I couldn't let it go. Every late-night business dinner or overnight trip after that, I was suspicious. It ate at me, and finally, neither of us could take it anymore. It was civil at first. He moved out, and we tried to do mediation. Split custody, split finances. All I wanted from him was child support to help pay for day care and essentials, but one day, during a meeting with the mediator, he let me in on another little secret of his. He'd collected Leia's DNA and had a paternity test done without my knowledge."

"And he wasn't the father."

"Nope."

"I thought it didn't matter to him?"

"So did I," she whispers.

"But it did."

"It did in the end. So much so that it drove him into the arms of other women—at least, that's the story he told in court. Painting me out to be a liar and a scammer who was just after his money. The son of a bitch was a broke college student when we met. Everything we had, we built together. I wasn't after anything. I loved the asshole."

"His fragile, self-important ego is what drove him to fuck one of his employees. Not you," I hiss.

"I know that," she agrees.

She attempts to touch my arm, and I move out of her reach.

Silence fills the space between us as I stare at this woman, who has spent almost every day with me for the last few months, yet never bothered to mention that the little girl I'd taught to fish and had a tea party with was my flesh and blood.

"Say something," she pleads.

"I'm processing."

"I'm sorry, Sebastian."

I fold my arms over my chest to keep from punching the wall as anger vibrates through me.

"For which part? Passing my baby off as someone else's?"

Her chin lifts, and her eyes blaze with indignation.

"I didn't know how to get in touch with you. I didn't have a phone number or address. I didn't even know your last name, for God's sake. What was I supposed to do?" she yells.

"What about the last four months, Avie? I've been right here. You had every opportunity to tell me."

Her eyes fall to the floor. "I was scared."

"Of what?" I roar.

"Of this. Of your reaction."

"So, protecting yourself was more important than letting me know that the little girl I've been bonding with is my fucking daughter?"

"No. Protecting *her.* I couldn't risk you rejecting her too. She was devastated and confused when Conrad just disappeared from her life. She adored him. He broke her heart, and I had to make sure you wouldn't do the same thing," she screams.

That's when my legs move, and I advance on her. She stands her ground and holds my eyes as I rant in frustration.

"That's a fucking cop-out, and you damn well know it. It was reckless and selfish. How long were you planning on playing this game? Till November? Were you gonna take off and never tell me?"

"I was going to tell you everything tonight."

I laugh in her face. "Sure you were."

"I was. That's why I wanted us to go somewhere alone after the festival. I told you I need to talk to you about something."

"Well, isn't that awfully convenient?"

"I'm sorry," she says again. "I didn't think I'd ever see you again. I didn't mean for any of this to happen."

"Didn't think or didn't want? Because there's a big difference."

"I'm sorry," she repeats.

"About which part?" I howl in her face.

"All of it."

I throw my hands in the air and stomp to the door.

"Where are you going?" she asks.

"Anywhere but here. I don't want to look at you right now."

I block out her guttural wails as I walk the fuck away.

"Sebastian."

I come to a halt when I hear Amiya's voice.

"Where's Leia?" I ask without turning to face her.

"With your grandparents."

I nod and start forward again.

"She loves you, you know."

At those words, I finally spin to meet her gaze.

"She's got a fucking funny way of showing it."

"You're right; it's all a big, ugly, gnarly fucking mess, and she didn't handle any of it correctly. You have every right to be angry. But you need to know that she wasn't trying to hurt or manipulate you. She doesn't have a manipulative bone in her body. Trust me, I've tried to find it and set it loose."

I glare at her. Not in the mood for her shit.

"It just got too big, and she didn't know how to dig her way out."

"Yeah, well, she buried herself."

Her eyes fill with disappointment, and she shakes her head.

"My God, you're exactly the man she was afraid you'd be."

With that blow, she twirls on her heel and walks away.

chapter forty

Avie

"Avie, time to get up, sunshine," Amiya says as she slings the curtains shading the bedroom window open.

I groan as I pull the pillow from under my head and hold it over my eyes.

She sits on the bed beside me. "I know you're sad or embarrassed or depressed or something."

"All of the above," I mumble.

"But you can't just hide under the covers. You have a job and a tiny human depending on you. So, get your ass out of this bed and into a shower, or I'm going to fucking drag you in there by your hair."

"I called in sick."

"For the third day in a row. Your boss had chicken soup and Gatorade delivered this morning. And Leia is worried to death about you."

I peek out from behind the pillow. "Where is she?"

"At Ida Mae's house, playing with the cat. I thought it'd be best in case I had to wrestle you to get you out."

"What did you tell her?"

"That you and Conrad had a disagreement and it made you sad."

I nod and push myself up against the headboard, and my body screams in protest. Everything hurts.

"You need to talk to Sabel as well. She's been by every day, asking after you and feeding me and Leia."

"I have no idea what to say to her and Sebby. I feel like I betrayed their kindness."

"Unfortunately, you made your bed, and now, it's time to lie in it. It's gonna suck, but it has to be done," she says.

"I know."

My body shakes as I begin to sob.

Amiya crawls up beside me and wraps me in her arms.

"I'll give you the rest of today to finish crying it out, but no longer."

I feel like a human again after eating and taking a long, hot shower.

Leia is thrilled when she finds me sitting at the kitchen island, eating toast. "Good morning, Mommy."

Guilt washes over me as she carefully hugs me.

"I feel much better, baby," I reassure her.

Amiya makes a pot of coffee, pours us each a mug, and slides one to me. She makes Leia a bowl of cereal.

I open my mouth to protest the sugary meal, but Amiya holds up her hand.

"We ran out of eggs, and that's the only thing I know how to cook other than toast. One morning won't hurt her."

"It's Bastian," Leia says around a mouthful.

I jerk my head around to peer out of the window and into the living room.

I don't see him.

"Where is Sebastian?" Amiya asks her.

She points to the cereal box on the island with her spoon.

"Cap'n Crunch," she says.

Amiya picks up the box and examines it.

"I can see it. They're both old and goofy."

Leia giggles.

When she makes it to the bottom of her bowl, she picks it up and slurps the remaining milk. Amiya takes the bowl and places it in the sink.

"Okay, kid, go brush your teeth and find your bathing suit. You and I are going to the beach while Mommy works."

Leia hops down and skips to her room.

"So, what's the plan?" Amiya asks once Leia is out of earshot.

"I'm going to talk to Kimball this morning and tender my resignation. Talk to Sabel and ask if I can break my lease two months early. Call my parents and ask if Leia and I can stay with them for a while. Then, I'm going to have a realtor list the loft. It's time for us to start over. Again."

She leans her elbows on the granite in front of me. "Not that it doesn't thrill me to have you back in Atlanta, but don't you think you should at least stay here until the end of your contract?"

I shake my head. "I can't be here."

"What about Sebastian?" she asks.

"What about him?"

"The cat's out of the bag now. You can't put it back in. No matter how badly you want to. He's not just gonna let you take off with Leia," she whispers.

"Has he been here the last three days?" I ask.

"What?"

"Has he shown up here at all the last three days?" I ask slowly.

"No, but …"

"But nothing, Amiya. All us being here has done is complicate his life. I'm sure, at this point, he wishes we'd never come to Sandcastle Cove."

"Don't pretend you're running away for his benefit."

"I'm not running away."

"Who do you think you're talking to? I know you," she quips.

"Amiya, please. Please don't."

She stands and backs away. "Fine. You know I'll always have your back. You run, and I run with you."

I help her get Leia ready for their day and wait until the Mercedes is backing out of the driveway before getting dressed.

Grabbing my keys and purse, I open the front door to find Sabel standing on the stoop, wringing her hands.

"Hi. I was just about to knock," she says.

Tears prick at the back of my eyes when I see her.

"Oh, Avie," she says as she wraps her arms around me.

She lets me cry on her shoulder for several minutes before she coaxes me across the street for a cup of tea.

I wait on the deck as she goes inside. Returning with steaming mugs.

She hands one to me and takes the seat beside me.

"I'm sorry, Sabel. You and Sebby have been so kind to us, and I never meant to hurt you. Any of you."

She doesn't say anything as she lays her hand on mine and lets me do all the talking.

"I didn't set out to deceive you. I had no idea that you were Sebastian's grandparents. I had no idea that he lived in Sandcastle Cove, not until the day I found him and Sebby in the garden, working on the tree house. I was in shock when I realized he was the boy I'd met in Hawaii. I never thought I'd see him again. I know that I should have told him about Leia right then, but I couldn't speak."

My eyes flicker from our hands to her face.

"There's no excuse for not telling you. I panicked. And then, after the initial shock wore off, I kept intending to have the conversation with Sebastian. It just never seemed to be the right time, and then too much time passed, and I didn't know how because I ..." I bow my head as I realize the truth. "I fell for him, and I was afraid to lose him."

Reckless. Selfish. He was right.

"I planned to come clean the night he found out, but Conrad beat me to it. I honestly did plan to, but Sebastian doesn't believe me, and I don't blame him."

"He's a stubborn boy. Always has been. He gets it from his grandfather," she says. "He's not good at communicating his feelings. Be patient."

I shake my head. "It's too late."

"Oh, dear girl, as long as you're both still breathing, it's never too late."

"You don't hate me?" I whisper.

She pats my hand. "How can I hate the woman who gave me such a wonderful great-grandbaby?"

A sob escapes me.

"We all make mistakes in life, Avie. Some are bigger than others. What matters is what we do to make it right."

"I don't know how to make this right," I admit.

"That's why I brought you over here. Ida Mae always says there's nothing you can't figure out over a cup of tea. So, let's get to figuring."

chapter forty-one

Sebastian

"JUST GOT OFF THE PHONE WITH YOUR GRANDMOTHER," GRAMPS says as I arrive for the day.

"Is there more to that story?" I ask when he fails to continue.

"She was crying. I can't stand to hear a woman cry. Makes me feel helpless."

Women's tears aren't exactly my favorite thing either.

"Avie visited her this morning. Apologized for everything and asked if she could break her lease."

I figured she'd head back to New York.

"We're gonna miss our little great-granddaughter," he states.

Great-granddaughter.

The weight of those words hit me like a ton of bricks. Leia is their great-granddaughter. My parents' granddaughter. *My* little girl. I grab a brush and start scrubbing the interior of the vessel.

"Easy, son. You're gonna peel the leather off the bench," Gramps says.

"You want to do it yourself, old man?"

"No. I just don't want you to take your battling emotions out on my ship."

I toss the brush in the bucket and stand to face him. "What am I supposed to do, Gramps? If you were me, would you beg her to stay to make Mom and Nana happy? Forget the fact that she withheld my daughter from me? Pretend like it wasn't all a game to her?"

"I'd simply ask myself if I'd be happy if I never saw the woman I was in love with again. If I'd be happy to never see my child again. Because this isn't about your mom or your grandmother. This is about you and *your* family."

My family.

Possessiveness blooms inside me.

"I don't know if I can trust her."

"That's fair. I'd have a hard time trusting a gal who put her child's happiness and well-being ahead of her own too."

"How was keeping Leia from me putting her first?"

"You were a stranger, son. To both of them. A mother protects her cubs from strangers."

"I'm her dad."

"It takes a lot more than planting a seed to be a dad, son. She took her time vetting you. Now, in a perfect world, she'd have done that before deciding to have a child with you, but we don't live in a perfect world. The baby came first, and then she had to get to know you. I'm not saying it was right or wrong. I'm just trying to help you see the reasons she made the choices she made. Taking her time to learn what kind of man you are, opening her heart, and risking it first before letting you have access to Leia's heart. Allowing Leia to fall in love with you naturally because she wanted to and not because she was told you were her father and she had to."

"Fuck," I roar as I kick the bucket across the deck. "I don't know what to do, Gramps. I'm so damn angry, but I do love them. I want them."

"Well then, go tell her that."

"You make it sound simple."

"It's words strung together. It doesn't get much simpler than that."

"I'm gonna need the day off."

He grins and slaps me on the back. "I'll have your mom dock your paycheck."

I race to the cottage, fueled by desire and rage. I have no plan and no idea what I'm going to say, but I've spent the last three days trying to come up with something and couldn't, so I just have to wing it.

I park on the road, sprint to the front door, and knock. She doesn't open for me, but I see the curtains shift, and I know she's in there. I hop off the stoop and go around the side of the house. I climb the steps to the screened-in porch that leads to the kitchen.

The sliding doors are locked.

I beat my fist against the glass.

"Answer the door, Avie!"

She peeks around the wall from the living room. "Go away, Sebastian," she calls.

"Not until you talk to me."

She disappears, and I start pounding the glass harder.

"I swear to God, I'll break this door," I bellow.

"Stop it," she yells as she reappears and makes her way over to face me. "Are you drunk?" she asks, anger sparking in her eyes.

"No, I'm not drunk."

"You're acting like it. I'm not going to talk to you while you're acting like a Neanderthal."

I lay my head against the door. "You're pissed at me," I murmur.

"No, I'm not," she says.

I look up at her. "Yes, you are. You're pissed I haven't been there for you and her."

She shakes her head as a tear slides down her cheek.

I tap my head against the glass.

"You're pissed when I didn't even know she existed."

She whimpers as she leans her head against mine, the glass separating us.

"Fuck, Avie. That's not fucking fair."

"I know," she whispers.

"Let me in," I plead.

A few agonizing moments pass before I hear the lock click and she steps back.

I slide the door open and step inside.

She turns and walks to the refrigerator and removes a pitcher of iced tea as she gestures for me to sit.

She fills two glasses and sits down beside me.

I stare at her.

She's beautiful. Even with her puffy, red-rimmed eyes and splotchy face.

I want to reach out and cup her face. To kiss the sadness away, but I don't. There's too much to be said before I can touch her.

She slides one of the teas to me. "There's nothing that can't be figured out over a cup of tea," she says cryptically.

chapter forty-two

Sebastian

I TAKE A DEEP BREATH AND LOOK OVER HER SHOULDER, WHERE MY eyes focus on a stack of boxes on the floor.

"What are those?" I ask, and her eyes follow mine.

"Packing boxes," she says.

"Why the fuck are you packing?"

"This isn't our home, Sebastian," she murmurs.

"It could be," I say.

She turns back to me. "No, it's just somewhere we spent the summer. It's time we get back to our life."

"Our life. Leia is four years old. Her life is wherever the people she loves are."

"Sebastian."

"You can't tell me you don't love Sandcastle Cove. I know she does."

She shakes her head.

"Fuck, Avie. You guys landed on my island for a reason. Can't you see that? She belongs here with us, with me. You both do. I know things are fucked up right now, and I said a lot of shit in anger the other night. But we can figure it out if you stay."

"I can't. I can't let someone else hurt her," she cries.

"Her or you?"

"Either of us," she says as she pushes away from the island and stands.

I grasp her hand before she can run.

"Hey, I love you."

"It doesn't matter," she says.

"Why not?"

"Because we were told that before and it didn't matter."

"Conrad. This is about Conrad," I say, anger flaring again.

"Yes, it is. He said those words, and then he took them back. I can take that blow again, but not Leia. She can't lose another …"

The words die on her lips as she looks away from me.

"Father. Say it."

Her eyes snap back to me. "She can't lose another father. That's not fair to her. I can't let her love you."

I stand, step into her, and lean down so we're eye to eye. "Too late. She already does love me, and I love her."

A whimper bubbles in her throat. "How do I trust that?"

"Do something for me. Separate how you felt about Conrad and what he said he felt about you, and tell me how Conrad made you feel."

Her chest heaves as she chokes back a sob.

"You loved him, right? He said he loved you, right?"

"Yes."

"Okay, but did you feel loved? Did he make you laugh? Did he tell you how fucking beautiful you were every day? What an incredible mother you were? Did he run home as fast as he could so he could eat dinner with you? Even when the long day had kicked his ass. Did he want to rest in between the two of you? Did he read Leia to sleep and tuck her in so she felt safe and secure at night? Did he hold you when you drifted off to sleep? Did he do even the bare minimum to show you that he loved you?"

"No."

"Any man can say the words, Avie. Doesn't mean that he feels them. I'm sorry he lied to you, but that's on him, not me. I love you, both of you, Avie. You and Leia. I love you both. You're my family. Can't you feel it?" I ask as I reach over and tuck a stray strand of hair behind her ear. My hand slides down to cradle her cheek.

Tears begin to stream down her face as she leans into my palm and the words penetrate.

"Please. Stay."

She shakes her head. "I turned in my notice. I don't have a job anymore or anywhere to live. I ..."

"Do you love me?"

"Sebastian."

"Just answer the fucking question. Do you love me?"

"Yes," she whispers.

"That's all that matters. The rest is just details. We'll figure everything else out. Together. Stay."

She closes her eyes for a brief moment and I hold my breath as I wait for her to speak.

"Okay," she whispers.

The word is a balm, and I bring my other hand to her face and pull her to me. I swallow her cries as I cover her mouth with mine.

All of the confusion and anger melt as I kiss away her fear.

"Well, well, well, this is an interesting development."

I lift my eyes as Avie breaks away and looks over her shoulder.

Amiya is standing in the doorway, watching us above her lowered sunglasses with a wicked grin on her face.

"Warning: your daughter is on her way inside, and you two have some explaining to do," she says as she walks to the island and drops the beach bag she's carrying. "The little bugger is smarter than she lets on, and she's been quizzing me on what went down at the wharf. She saw you screaming at her mother."

"What did you tell her?" Avie asks.

"I told her that her mommy and daddy were going to explain it all to her. That's you two, by the way," she quips.

Avie's eyes come to me. "Are you ready for this?" she asks.

"Yeah, let's go talk to our little girl."

We find Leia out front. She's in the tire swing Gramps and I hung. Her fists are wrapped around the ropes, and she's spinning in the wind.

"Hi, kiddo," I say as I reach up and still the swing.

"Bastian, you're here!" she cries before leaping down from the tire and wrapping her arms around my legs. "I thought you were mad at us."

My heart squeezes at her words. I'm such a dick for making her worry.

I go to a knee and look her in the eye. "I'm sorry I made you think I was upset. I was never mad at you."

"Are you mad at Mommy?" she asks.

"I was."

"Why?"

"It's a long story. Maybe we should put on our fairy wings and talk about it like adults while we have a tea party," I suggest.

She considers me for a moment, and then she looks up at Avie. "You too?"

Avie smiles. "Yeah, me too."

We each take her by the hand and lead her to the garden. And there, over a cup of imaginary tea, the two of us gently explain how we met all those years ago on a breathtaking beach in Hawaii. How she was made from our instant love and how we lost each other and couldn't find one another again until divine intervention brought them to my island.

She's confused, and it doesn't make sense to her, but in the end, she grasps that I am going to be her daddy now, that I love her very much, and that we are going to be a family.

And that's enough for her.

It's enough for me too.

My girls.

chapter forty-three

Avie

I leave Sebastian and Leia among the flowers. He has her by the waist and is holding her above his head as he runs around, helping her "fly."

My heart swells watching his strong hands carefully handle her and then nearly explodes as her joyful laughter echoes through the garden.

Home.

In that moment I know that Sandcastle Cove is home.

I climb the steps to the back porch where I find Amiya waiting for me on the outdoor sofa with a glass of wine in hand.

She scooches over and I sit down beside her.

"We're staying," I say as I snatch the glass from her fingers and take a sip.

She grins. "I knew you were all along. I've just been waiting for you to figure it out."

"I need to call Kimball and retract my resignation and hope she'll still recommend me for the permanent position here on the island. And I'll have to find us somewhere to live since our lease is up in November," I babble.

Amiya chuckles.

"I'm sure you'll be able to work something out with Sebby and Sabel. After all, you are their great-granddaughter's mother. Might as well start using the little crumb snatcher to your advantage," she teases.

I pull a decorative pillow from behind my back and hurl it at her. She artfully dodges my assault.

"I'm proud of you," she says as she stretches out her hand.

So am I.

"Proud enough to babysit for me one more night before you leave for Alanta?" I ask.

"Hot date?"

I grin.

"I have a couple of debts to pay off, and Sebastian is calling in his markers."

She rolls her eyes. "Ugh, you're such a slut."

"So, is that a yes?"

"Of course."

I lay my head on her shoulder. "I love you."

"I love you too."

epilogue

Sebastian

Three Months Later

"I'VE HIRED A CONTRACTOR," I TELL AVIE AS SHE REMOVES groceries from the brown paper bag and puts them away.

"For what?"

"To help finish the renovations on the house."

She stops what she's doing and turns to look up at me.

"Why?"

I shrug.

"I'm slow and learning my way on YouTube. It'll take forever to get everything finished at that rate, especially the bathroom addition. So I talked to Lennon's best friend, Wade Lusk. He owns a contracting business on the island, and he has time in his schedule."

"But I thought you wanted to do it yourself."

I make my way around the island to her. My hands settle on her hips and I tug her in close.

"I did, but if I continue to do it all, it will be another six months before it's ready for us to move in."

She sighs and her eyes flutter shut as my lips find her throat.

"You don't need to take on the added expense on our account. But if you really want to do this, let me contribute to some of the costs. I have my money from selling the properties up north."

"I'm not taking your money," I whisper into her ear, "It's purely selfish. I want my girls under the same roof as me."

She moans as my teeth graze her earlobe.

"Besides, Wade is giving me the family discount," I assure her.

Thank goodness.

My mind drifts to the ring being sized at Sea Goddess Jewelers as I pepper kisses across her jaw.

The front door opens, and the click of tap shoes make their way from the living room.

"Mommy, Daddy!" Leia bellows as she bursts into the kitchen with Nana on her heels.

"Look what Miss Eden taught us today."

She shuffles clumsily on the wood floor and we clap as she finishes.

"I told her she shouldn't wear the tap shoes outside of class but she refused to take them off until she showed you two," Nana informs.

I scoop her up and kiss her cheek.

"My little star."

Leia

Three Months Later

I'm sitting on the counter beside the stove. Daddy is cooking dinner, and he's letting me help. I stir the big pot while he adds all the things.

"What are we making?" I ask.

"Frogmore stew."

I wrinkle my nose. "We're having frogs for dinner? Gross!"

He laughs. "There are no frogs in it. Only shrimp and sausage. This was my favorite thing your grandma Milly made for me and Uncle Lennon when I was your age."

"I like shrimps."

He taps the tip of my nose. "Just like your daddy."

I smile. I like being just like him.

He lives on the beach but always has dinner with us- and tucks me in bed- before he goes home at night. Sometimes he has a sleepover with Mommy and I hear him sneak out before the light comes up in the morning, but I don't say anything. I like it when he stays. Nana says one day we will all live together, I just have to be patient. It's hard.

The soup begins to bubble and he adds the shrimp to the pot when Mommy runs into the kitchen, waving her phone in the air.

"I got a text. The turtle nest at the Thirty-Second Street access is boiling!" she says.

"Boiling? It's fifty degrees out tonight," Daddy says.

"Boiling means hatching, silly," I squeal as I hop down and sprint to the front door to grab my shoes.

We get to see the baby turtles tonight.

"Hatching?"

"Yes, come on. We have to go to the beach," I tell him.

"I guess the stew will have to wait," Daddy mumbles and turns off the stove.

Mommy rummages through the drawers in the kitchen and finds flashlights. She hands them to Daddy and asks him to add the red things on them.

Nana comes in the back door with Ida Mae.

"This is so exciting," Nana gasps.

"Are you coming to see the babies, too?" I ask.

"We sure are," she says.

Nana helps me into my coat, and we all get into Daddy's Bronco.

The baby turtles dig out of the sand.

"They're so little," I say as I watch another one and another one climb out. "Will their mommy come and get them?" I ask Nana.

She shakes her head.

"No. They're going to have to find their own way home, and we're going to help them. Come. Let's light their way."

Nana, Ida Mae, and I stand near the water and turn on our flashlights.

Mommy stands at the top of the nest, but her flashlight is red.

The turtle babies start turning around in the sand and walking toward us.

"They're coming," Nana gasps.

We watch as each one floats out to the sea to find their family, just like Mommy and I found ours.

I say a prayer and then whisper to the babies.

"I hope you find them."

acknowledgments

2024. Are you guys as excited for the new year as I am? Lots of great things are in the works. We had the Poplar Falls box sets released in February. The fifth-anniversary cover of the Cross My Heart Duet was released on my five-year publishing anniversary. And now, we have the first book in a brand-new series. I hope you guys enjoyed your introduction to the coastal small town of Sandcastle Cove, North Carolina. I can't wait for you all to get to know the residents on a deeper level as we continue the series.

There are lots of people to thank for their contribution to this book.

Autumn Sexton, you're the whole package. A mentor, a task-master, a masterful publicist, alpha reader, brainstorming partner, teaser savant, therapist, and best friend. Oh, how I look forward to seeing where we go together this year.

My brilliant editor, Jovana Shirley, is the one who takes my words and helps craft them into the beautiful story that you guys receive. We are a team in the most fundamental definition of the word. There is no book without her. I love you, Jo, and commas are the devil.

Sommer Stein, you take my vision for covers and bring it to life. It's uncanny how in sync we are. You take my vague thoughts and make art. Beautiful, breathtaking art.

Judy Zweifel, your keen eye catches everything that gets by the rest of us. You're the best cleanup crew, and you're so gracious to always find a way to fit me into your very tight schedule. Thank you.

Stacey Blake, your interiors are always on point and convey the mood of the story. You're fast, accommodating, and such a delight. I so enjoy working with you.

I want to shout out Kyla Linde for organizing the Aloha Anthology. The short story I submitted to support the charity that benefited the Maui Food Bank and Maui Fire Relief Fund was the catalyst for what became The Sandcastle Cove Series. We raised $66,000 dollars for the island, and I'm so proud. I love you and your big heart, Tiny Dancer.

Also need to acknowledge my stunning island home of Oak Island, which serves as the inspiration for Sandcastle Cove. The residents, the small-town vibes, the community, and the beauty of this magical place are all woven into the pages of this book.

I want to thank you, the readers, for following me into a new world. You guys are the best and the reason I get to live my dream. Words are not adequate to express my gratefulness.

Last but not least, I want to thank my ever-patient, steadfast, supportive, and sexy husband, David, for being my rock in this crazy ride called life. I'd marry you again every day. Even the ones when I want to strangle you.

other books

Cross My Heart Duet

Both of Me

Both of Us

Poplar Falls

Rustic Hearts

Stone Hearts

Wicked Hearts

Fragile Hearts

Merry Hearts

Crazy Hearts

Knitted Hearts

Lake Mistletoe Series

Lake Mistletoe

Smitten in Lake Mistletoe

Stranded in Lake Mistletoe

The Balsam Ridge Series

Life After Wife

Fate After Fame

Rain After Fire

Hope After Loss

Rise After Fall

Cozy After Snow

about the author

Amber Kelly is a romance author that calls North Carolina home. She has been a avid reader from a young age and you could always find her with her nose in a book completely enthralled in an adventure. With the support of her husband and family, in 2018, she decided to finally give a voice to the stories in her head and her debut novel, Both of Me was born. You can connect with Amber on Facebook at facebook.com/AuthorAmberKelly, on IG @authoramberkelly, on twitter @AuthorAmberKel1 or via her website www.authoramberkelly.com..

Printed in Great Britain
by Amazon

45915404R00175